WRONG PLACE, WRONG TIME

A STORY OF PIRACY AND POLITICAL INTRIGUE FROM AFRICA TO WHITEHALL

RAY CROWE

authorHOUSE®

AuthorHouse™ UK
1663 Liberty Drive
Bloomington, IN 47403 USA
www.authorhouse.co.uk
Phone: UK TFN: 0800 0148641 (Toll Free inside the UK)
*   UK Local: (02) 0369 56322 (+44 20 3695 6322 from outside the UK)*

Published by AuthorHouse 11/12/2021

ISBN: 978-1-6655-9465-3 (sc)
ISBN: 978-1-6655-9466-0 (e)

Two young people get drawn into a multi-million pound piracy operation on their honeymoon cruise. They see too much and so the hunt begins. They have allies in high places. They also have enemies who know their every move.

When Belle is kidnapped can Felix reach her before it's too late?

Who can they trust in Whitehall?

CHAPTER 1

The thick sea mist hung like a silver curtain over the Lincolnshire fens. Felix tried to peer through the windows out into the grim dark night and was amazed when he checked his watch that it was not yet four o'clock.

It was an early January afternoon on the East Coast and the rain sodden mist and gloom were not by any means out of the ordinary.

He quickly checked the monitors that covered one side of the living room wall. Each was showing a mass of distorted shapes as the receptors on the units were unable to produce any coherent images in the horrendous weather conditions.

He had spent weeks carefully placing these sensors on all of the possible access points to the windmill. He had also placed infra-red movement sensors across footpaths and the only road that approached the mill. He had fitted microwave operated technology CCTV that surrounded the perimeter. This required no wiring and was operated purely on the emission of microwaves being beamed back to a receiver. This technology was supposed to be impervious to extreme weather conditions.

He looked around at the collection of security equipment. The wall cupboard full of high-powered sniper rifles with the latest infra-red night vision sites attached. These were alongside various automatic and semi-automatic hand-guns, machine guns and a collection of explosives, including stun grenades and the latest selection of state of the art weaponry.

He checked the main door to the Windmill and everything seemed okay. Yet again he checked his high-powered radio receiver but only to be greeted by a stony silence. The land line was of course out of action and even his mobile phone was registering no signal.

1

Nobody would try anything on a night like this he thought, the logistics alone would make it impossible to move around in fenland terrain that is a nightmare in good weather.

The treacherous channels that blend into the rye grass as if camouflaged can be steep banked and incredibly slippery. Even at low tide they hold a glutinous black oily substance that even experienced local fen men have been known to perish in.

With the tide rushing in the sea mist being swirled into dense patches the driving rain reducing vision to arm's length if you are lucky, no this was not the right time or the right place to see the demise of Felix Barnard.

So if all of this was indeed the case, why did he have this premonition of impending doom?

This sixth sense had kept him alive before so he had learned to treat it with respect.

Felix ran up the circular stairs to the top floor that had been converted from its original drive shaft housing for the sails, to a lookout position fitted with high power infra-red binoculars and a selection of high specification scanning system. He checked the hundred metre perimeter ground censors but the weather conditions were causing the readings to be questionable. There was no sign of movement or body heat on any of the surveillance equipment.

Felix returned to the large L shaped lounge that had been built on the side of the main building on the ground floor and made an instant decision, based on instinct alone, and quickly selected a Glock 23 pistol, a FM Minimi light machine gun, a handful of stun grenades, night vision glasses and a hunting knife from the cupboards on the walls.

He remembered his training at Hereford and the short, tough wiry Glaswegian Sergeant's last words "Trust your instinct laddie" he growled as he crushed his fingers in a farewell handshake. All the facts pointed to their being no danger but his gut reaction was to get out now. He quickly looked round at the sparse but comfortably furnished living accommodation that had served as home for the last few months, "So it begins" he said out loud. He placed all the items into his backpack and made for the fireplace.

CHAPTER 2

H e pulled back the large rug, from in front of the fireplace, and entered the tunnel he had dug himself, four months ago, for just this eventuality. Once he had entered the tunnel he removed the lightweight paving slab with its ring pull, and replaced it with a full thickness slab, which he slotted into the floor frame and locked into place from beneath. Under this he slid another full size slab to ensure there were no tell-tale hollow sounds when checked from above.

The tunnel was only around three hundred metres long, enough to reach a deep sided but shallow channel, at the rear of the Windmill. Housed at the end of the tunnel and covered by bracken was a shallow flat bottomed canoe. The channel, which retained water at all times, led to a boathouse concealed about another five hundred metres away.

The roof of the boathouse was built of carbon fibre covered in layers of soil and salt grass. Over the months since its construction many fen land plants had grown voraciously on this new domain and it had blended totally into the environment.

The entrance from the front was concealed by training the natural foliage to grow like a curtain over the entrance, this it had done with such vigour that it had become necessary to prune the growth back after a few weeks.

The camouflage had become so effective that Felix had watched a team of plant biologists from Lincoln University actually standing on the roof collecting samples for analysis.

If outside was all as nature intended the inside was quite the opposite. The water in the entrance never fell below two metres, even at low tide, and rose around three metres on a normal tide and up to four metres on a spring tide. This meant the two craft that were concealed in the boathouse had to be raised quite a distance to keep them clear of the brackish and very high salt content water at all times.

The walls of the boathouse on the inside were also made of carbon fibre covered in camouflage netting to reduce glare and any sound permeating the still of the fens where sound travel miles.

The first craft was a ten metre Neil Watson 36 inshore fishing smack. She had a comfortable cabin below the fully enclosed cockpit and was fitted with the Johansson trawl net hoist, originally invented by the Vikings; she was aptly named *Lincoln Belle*. His wife was called Belle by all her close friends. The cabin was fully stocked with provisions and carried enough extra fuel for a continuous week of sailing.

On the surface just the sort of fishing smack you would expect to see either off shore or exploring the salting's. Below the surface it was equipped with; a depth charge launcher, hidden in the Johansson hoist, and a selection of depth charge torpedoes. The original Volvo engine was replaced with a Cummins 6CTA 480hp marine series allowing the smack to touch thirty knots this being achieved one cold night in January at two in the morning at the edge of the Wash.

It also had the latest marine GPS navigation system and a computerised communication system which included an automatic pilot system.

The second craft had no pretence to be other than what it was, it had a long pointed bow that was raised at the prow, the rest of the craft was a sleek shape designed to maximise every aspect of its air dynamics and reduce its coefficient of drag. It did have a small cockpit that was below the highline of the hull but even this had been designed not to interfere with its primary function, speed. It was powered by a massive Kawasaki 135hp marine engine and had a top speed of forty knots, again achieved on a quiet winters evening off the Lincolnshire coast, which caused Felix's ankles to ache for days afterwards. This craft had no weapons no gadgets just raw power and speed and it was a last throw of the dice option if other methods had failed.

When Felix reached the boathouse he checked his tell-tales he had left at the entrance to the tunnel, he aimed his laser beam at the external sensors and none showed any activity.

He still moved quietly around the boathouse activating the hoist on the Neil Watson which lowered almost totally silently due to the special silicon coated ropes on the well-oiled shackles and davits. The Lincoln Belle slipped gently into the black murky water and Felix looped the bow ropes through the mooring hitch. He went through his well-practised procedure of preparing her for the agitated and angry sea that awaited her.

Although he had planned for this moment the reality that it may have actually arrived made him nervous. Had he carried out his planned defensive strategy efficiently, or had he forgotten anything?

"Well if you haven't done it now it's too late to worry" he could hear his dad saying. "Guess your right dad" he said to a tin of Heinz beans. This never answered. He suddenly felt so alone with no one to share his fears.

He looked into the black fen water coated in the oily streaks emanating from the peat and it seemed to have a foreboding presence. It somehow seemed to be inviting him to jump in and escape from all of his worries.

"Come on grow up and get on with it" he said clenching his fists, this time addressing several empty fuel jerry cans.

CHAPTER 3

"*Belle would have loved this*" Felix thought as he pushed his curly brown hair out of his eyes, and carried all the essentials from the storeroom to the galley and the cabin. She always loved putting to sea in whatever craft they had. From their first tentative steps in their single sail Laser trainers in the rain at Old Portsmouth when they were twelve years old, to the thirty foot racing yacht they sailed from Christchurch only a few months ago. Was that really only eight months ago so much has happened since those carefree days? His mind wandered back. They had met at a junior sailing training day and got cold, wet, exhausted and exhilarated all at the same time. They learned their sailing together, even though they lived some seventy miles apart, by switching lessons on a monthly basis. He could see her now, her tousled blonde hair stunning blue eyes and that mischievous smiling face. Her full name was Arabella but all who knew her called her Belle.

His mind ran back to their early years and their beginnings.

Felix's father, Ray Barnard, was an aircraft engineer and his mother Petra, was a Sister at a local hospital. They had lived in Portsmouth for many years. He had a really happy upbringing and his home life had been full of laughter and he even got on well with his sister, Michelle, when they weren't trying to strangle each other. As they grew up he and Michelle became really good friends and she and Belle got on like a house on fire. Michelle also went to Portsmouth University and was in her last year of qualification to become a doctor. Both Felix and Michelle had a zest for life. He inherited his father's bizarre humour being based on *Monty Python* and the *Naked Gun* films and their predecessors *Police Squad* and also his sporting prowess.

Ray Barnard had played professional football for Bournemouth before an injury ended his career. His father had been a great supporter of Felix's sporting achievements and had always found time to watch him play whenever possible.

He had his mother's stunningly dark brown eyes, which stood out from under the same curly brown hair. He had also inherited her resourcefulness, determination and her very dry sense of humour.

Felix had attended a local comprehensive and achieved seven GCSE's and had gone on to study at Havant College to gain the required five GCSE A Levels to attend Portsmouth University. He gained a BA honours degree in Naval Architecture, a subject that his love for the sea and sailing, made the perfect choice. He loved College and University being a keen sportsman and even represented the University at football and badminton.

His interest in sport had allowed his six foot frame to fill out and he weighed around twelve stone, in old money, and his long legs made him quick to cover the ground. He was continually having to keep his curly hair trimmed closely otherwise it would engulf his head in a light brown cascade.

Felix loved his home town and his favourite place was Old Portsmouth, so named because it was the part of the city that had not changed since Lord Nelson's day. The narrow streets and the tall buildings transported him back to the days when press gangs would have roamed the streets, looking for unwilling volunteers to join His Majesty's Royal Navy. The bars would have been full of drunken sailors and revellers spilling out onto the cobbled streets. This part of the city was also called "Spice Island" due to the cargoes that were landed at the nearby Camber Docks.

The Still and West public house on the point was Felix and Belles favourite place to eat with views across the harbour to Gosport and the Naval Dockyard. Belle knew much of the local history of the area and it was she who explained to Felix that the pub was originally called 'The Still' but changed its name when the landlord's daughter married the landlord of the nearby 'East and West Country House' and became the 'Still and West Country House'. As years passed by it became shortened to its present name. He was always amazed by just how much local history she actually knew, she really was amazing.

Arabella Worthington's father, Neville Worthington, had his own small yacht building company and her mother Davinia Worthington did the book keeping for the family business. The family had moved to Lymington in the heart of the New Forest thirty years ago when her father opened his business. He had been a chartered Accountant based at a firm in Bagshott and had hated every minute of his time there. They finally decided to take a gamble and put their savings into, what was ostensibly his hobby, boatbuilding.

Her mother was also a chartered accountant and both her and her husband had become totally different people since their life changing gamble. The business was doing well and they were happier than they had ever been. Belle had taken her build from her mother around five foot six inches tall and natural blonde hair, which she wore at neck length. She weighed around ten stone and was very fit and nimble on her feet due to her very active life style. She also had a caring and supportive family and this made both she and her sister Lucinda confident but easy going with the need to laugh whenever possible.

Belle had attended Lymington High School and then onto Lyndhurst College before attending Exeter University where she gained her BA Honours degree in Geology. Belle enjoyed her time at college and University and made some good friends because of her caring and easy going nature. She joined the University drama group and appeared in several small roles in their productions over the three years. Felix was often called upon to rehearse her lines but instead of improving her classic interpretation it usually ended in hysterical laughter and this most probably was instrumental in Belle not being offered leading roles in productions. Felix started calling her "Am dram mam" and she responded by calling him "Roger Moore" the man who killed real acting. Apart from being good at acting Belle was also a very good musician and could play several instruments including the guitar and the flute.

After he and Belle first met they seemed to continually bump into each other at various sailing events along the South Coast. Slowly their relationship moved beyond just sailing and they became inseparable. Both families were overjoyed and they got on with their prospective in laws really well. They enjoyed holidays in Cornwall walking the rugged coastline and sailing the waters off of Padstow. They soaked up the sun in the Maldives as a reward following their degree successes and spent the whole time in the water. Although it was a stunningly beautiful island and had the whitest sands and a stunning blue sea it did not offer enough activity for Belle and Felix.

Felix started to work for the Admiralty in 2006, based at Bath, as a draughtsman after he left Portsmouth University, while Belle was employed as a geologist at the Fossil centre at Lyme Regis following her degree from Exeter University. Belle loved her job and was completely enthralled with the science of tracing forms of life that existed millions of years ago. She would take Felix along all the beaches of the Jurassic Coast from Durdle Door to Lulworth Cove and of course Lyme Regis. Always so excited whenever they found ammonites or the fish remains in the shale at Church Cliffs. Felix enjoyed his job and was given more and more confidential work to carry out and he learnt not to discuss his work even with Belle.

They fell in love completely over the following years and they missed each other dreadfully whenever they had to be apart and spent hours on the phone or on" Skype" each not wanting to be the one to say goodnight.

They were married in January 2009 at St Marys Church Portsea. They chose Portsmouth because that was where they met, and agreed to put their careers on hold put all their savings into the purchase, via Belle's dad, of a thirty foot racing yacht. They were both now experienced and qualified sailors, and planned to take a year off and sail around the world. It all seemed so simple at the time. They even named their yacht *Vida Nova* which meant "New Life" in Portuguese. "This is the start of a new life for us my lovely" he said holding her in his arms as they stood on the deck of their new home for the next year or so. Belle looked up at Felix and said "My life will always be with you" They kissed passionately and held each other tightly on the eve of their great adventure.

They sailed leisurely to Australia and moored up off the barrier reef off of Queensland where they dived and enjoyed the most amazing time of their life, a long way from the cold water of Portsmouth Harbour.

Although they were not well versed in scuba diving they soon learnt and they saw the most amazing coloured fish and marine life around the coral reef. And the coral itself was a myriad of stunning colours inhabited by anemones whose wafting fronds reached out with bright red and blue antenna. It was a spectacular dazzling display of amazing colour set against the beautiful coral background.

There were shoals of brightly coloured fish in their thousands swaying one way then the other causing waves of changing light reflections. They also saw crabs and lobsters, large eels and fast moving Tiger Sharks, Reef Sharks and finally the Silvertip Shark which swam just a little too close from Belle's perspective. "This is paradise" he said to Belle" Apart from the sharks" laughed Belle. They spent two weeks moored off the reef and it was only by making a determined effort that they did eventually weigh anchor and head for Hong Kong and the China Sea.

They spent their days sailing and swimming, sometimes doing a bit of fishing to supplement their diet and generally enjoying the freedom that sailing without any agenda can bring. They sat enjoying the sunset one evening and looked at the huge red ball in the sky as it disappeared into the sea "You realise that the sun has really gone already and that what we are seeing is only a reflection" he said knowingly "Reflection or not it certainly is stunning" she replied. "I never knew life could be this good "said Belle staring into the red haze. "Well you are with me" Felix replied laughing. The smile disappeared when he was hit on the head with a fender and he fell from his perch on the stern into the sea. He looked up at Belle from the water and said "I think I am falling for you" She laughed "You have fallen you mean".

Although they had known each other for many years the time they spent together in these idyllic surroundings really made them fully understand just how deep their feelings were. They swam together they sat and watched the sun go down together and they made love on deck in the cabin and in the cockpit. It was as if an invisible bond was being tied around their hearts that would never be torn apart. They had met their perfect lover in the perfect environment and nothing would ever separate them ever.

CHAPTER 4

Felix was brought back to reality by a barely perceptible change to the pitch of the background noise of the wind and the rain, he quickly went to one of the periscope monitors at the side of the boathouse. At first he thought it was his mind playing tricks? but the sound was getting nearer and louder. At first he thought it was an assault helicopter but there was no way that it could be deployed in these weather conditions.

After several sweeps of the terrain finally he saw a hooded light attached to an assault hovercraft skimming across the waters of the bay. To say it was skimming was not entirely correct, it was being buffeted by the sea wind and was snaking erratically towards the location of the boathouse. He left his lookout post and collected a heavy duty rifle with armour piercing shells from his arsenal in the storeroom.

He returned with the weapon and steadied himself to take aim at the now onrushing hovercraft. It was almost impossible to get a steady shot as the hovercraft was veering like a bucking horse as it approached. He was now resigned to the fact that he was never going to hit the target and that as soon as he missed he would give away his location and they would have him trapped. He steadied the weapon but suddenly he lost sight of the hovercraft which had veered left onto the fenlands to his right. He hurriedly ran to his view point on the right side of the boathouse and saw the hovercraft skewing its way towards the Windmill that had been his home for the last eight months.

Through his Infra-red Binoculars Felix watched as several fully kitted troopers disembarked from the hovercraft and started to fan out as support for the main strike team that headed to the windmill. He was just about to board when one of the troopers suddenly appeared out of the gloom and approached the boathouse. He was so close he was standing on the roof directly above him. He waited nervously and could hear the trooper on his radio coordinating his approach route. Felix gambled on one more look through his peephole, it seemed that the trooper was looking straight at him, just coincidence, Felix thought. He could clearly hear the sound of his boots on the boathouse roof, suddenly they stopped and all went silent.

Felix waited what seemed an eternity and moved toward the boathouses concealed entrance very slowly using a small mirror on a stick to check that the trooper had gone. This little Hereford training tip saved his life as the trooper was standing pointing his AK 40 assault rifle at the entrance. Felix quickly and silently moved to the rear of the boathouse and exited via the tunnel entrance. This brought him behind the trooper and he swiftly and deftly used his SAS hunting knife in the way he had been taught and the trooper's body was slid quietly into the fen water. Shaking like a leaf now Felix hurried back to the boathouse. Training was one thing in real life it was totally different, still he thought *they have got my Belle*. He hoped the trooper had not radioed in his location. Too late to worry now he thought.

He boarded the Lincoln Belle, now fully provisioned and fuelled and flicked the electric starter motor the Cummins purred into life and he gently opened the throttle to ease her out into the inlet channel. As the bow made its way into the channel and out of the protection of the boathouse she rolled twisted and tried to corkscrew into the right hand bank as the onrushing current tried to take her down. Felix fought with the tiller gunned the big powerful engines to overcome the pull of the tide and the wind, he felt her come about as the twin propellers thrusted her forward. Slowly he was making way against the best the elements could throw at him and the sturdy built Lincoln Belle started to gain momentum.

He looked back towards the Windmill, there were torch lights flashing around the perimeter of the house, just about time to activate some defence weaponry that he had planned for the last eight months as he knew this day would come eventually.

Firstly he managed to activate the perimeter mines while still struggling with holding the Lincoln Belle on course within a minute the sky was lit up as angry tongues of flame spat into the sky lighting up the sodden landscape. Felix hoped his attackers would think this defence strategy was being orchestrated from within the windmill as he gunned the Neil Martin out into open water. The next stage of his defence strategy of the Windmill was self-activating relying on laser beams and photo electric cells to activate the charges.

As he navigated the narrow channel from the boathouse there were a more explosions, one even lighting up the sky momentarily, and then all fell silent.

As he opened up the throttle even more, the Lincoln Belle which was far more at home in these conditions than a hovercraft, surged its way into the River Welland. Here the river was fighting its own battle with the incoming tide as it tried to flow out to sea but the tide was forcing it back inland. The Lincoln Belle made slow but steady progress into the shallow reaches of the Wash. The next step was to avoid the sandbanks at Bulldog Sand and Breast Sand, which were submerged at high tide, and to tack to starboard using the lightship at the entrance to the Lynn channel as a backup to the navigational pilot that was programmed especially for these types of shallow estuary navigation conditions.

Felix had sailed these waters many times but never ever took anything for granted as the sea greeted fools with open arms. Slowly the lightship faded away to the starboard side as Felix now fought the cross current caused by three rivers and the five sandbanks that fought for dominance over the power of the incoming North Sea and then there was nothing other than the sound of the wind and rain and the crashing sea.

Eventually an hour later the dim lights of Hunstanton could be seen through the mist on the starboard bow and the Lincoln Belle made its way southerly on the freezing cold North Sea. Felix was now able to go below and engage the automatic pilot, it was only then he realised just how cold and wet he had become over the last two and a half hours. Although he had been in the cockpit, in the treacherous waters of the Wash with a force seven blowing and the tide running full you needed eyes all around you and he had been continually checking the draft visually. He put a kettle on the stove warmed his hands by the flame and switched on his digital radio transceiver, there would be a local shipping forecast at seven o clock only fifteen minutes to wait. As he poured out a steaming mug of coffee a news bulletin began. There was a massive explosion reported at a windmill some four miles from Fosdyke and it appeared there had been several serious casualties and some fatalities. As of yet it was not clear what had caused the explosion but a spokesman for the Lincolnshire Police had intimated it may have been a natural disaster suggesting a gas escape from the peaty soil. Felix hugged his mug and laughed out loud a natural gas explosion only goes to show how much control hidden forces have over the media.

You read and hear exactly what they want you to hear.

He looked at his mobile phone how he would have liked to have a reassuring chat with his mum and dad and let them know what was happening but he knew he couldn't.

If only he could talk to Belle just to let her know he had not abandoned her and that he was doing the best he could. He wanted to tell her he missed her with such a longing it had turned into physical pain in his chest. He knew he couldn't call Hutchins as there was a communication black out.

For the second time in a few hours he felt as if the world had abandoned him and that all the cares of the world were piled onto his shoulders. *"I can't do this"* he cried out to the North Sea. *"I don't know how"* he said banging the map table. In the midst of this dark wet night he heard his mother's voice in his head say "We believe in you son, we always have" Felix slowly smiled *"I know you have and I won't let you down."*

CHAPTER 5

His mind meandered back to Belle and their great adventure as they left the West coast of Australia in April 2009 and sailed the China Seas. They saw the stunning Hong Kong harbour and tasted the most amazing street cooked food restaurants or *Dai Pai Dongs* as they are known, They ate on Temple Street next to the market and had Cantonese food at Haiphong Street another day. No trip to Hong Kong would be complete without a trip on the Hong Kong tram and Felix and Belle toured the city saw all its best sights and returned to Vida Nova exhausted. They visited Wong Tai Sin temple and met many wonderful and friendly people. From there they sailed the Indian Ocean and made a special visit to Colombo in Srilanka. Felix's grandfather was stationed there during the Second World War, being a Shipwright in Portsmouth Dockyard he was called up into the Royal Navy as a Petty Officer as repair stations were set up around the world to carry out emergency repairs to Her Majesties warships. The real paradox was that while he was working in the naval dockyard, they were bombed continually and when he was called up for active service in 1942, he never saw or heard an enemy for the rest of the war. Although it was called Ceylon in his grandfather's days, the Srilankan people were the happiest people they had ever met: they smiled from dusk to dawn. Felix took Belle to a cricket match to watch Colombo play Mumbai, he was enthralled she was underwhelmed. They enjoyed the different types food available from Indian, English, Portuguese Asian and even McDonalds available.

They sailed on toward the West coast of Africa aiming to visit Nairobi. To reach Nairobi they had to sail the Indian Ocean off Mogadishu.

Two small launches approached selling local wares and they were waving their goods in the air as they came alongside. They had such welcoming smiling faces they hove to.

They came alongside apparently to show their wares and they were foolish enough to allow them aboard. Suddenly the smiles vanished and they were armed with an array of the latest issue of rifles and handguns.

They were taken ashore and their beloved Vida Nova was towed in by their captors.

They were taken to a small corrugated iron hut with a straw roof and the door was locked securely. They were kept there for a couple of days, time seemed to lose any meaning. The days were blisteringly hot and the nights were very humid.

Felix and Belle were shocked, frightened and taken completely unawares. Their idyllic existence had made them drop their guard and both had heard the grisly stories of hostages being taken by pirates and never being heard of again.

"I am so sorry" said Felix "I cannot believe how stupid I was" he continued putting his hands on Belles shoulders.

"I was as stupid as you" she said softly "Allowing ourselves to be boarded off the coast of Somalia" she laughed acidly. "How naïve could we be."

"Well let's see if we can find a way out of here" Felix said.

"I wish I had your optimism" she said sadly.

"When you're in a hole the only way is up" he said.

She smiled despite herself and said "What's the plan Houdini?"

Let's see how the land lies so we can formulate a plan" he said quietly.

Belle was now laughing out loud "I've ended up in the great escape!"

They now both started to laugh although they knew they were in deep trouble they at least had each other.

They were fed some dry maize and a small cup of water once a day via a slot in the metal door. Other than this their captors generally ignored them, treating them as some kind of investment.

On the third day they were visited by a tall grey haired Arab dressed in a white flannel suit that had obviously seen better days. He introduced himself as Achmed and said he had come to broker their release. He said he was not a part of the kidnapping group but here to act as a go between with all interested parties.

He then proceeded to photograph them, with his rather bulky camera, as they held a copy of some local newspaper dated 2 May 2009. They asked how long these negotiations could take at which he shrugged his shoulders and spread his hands in a gesture known all over the world.

"Maybe tomorrow maybe next year" he said without malice and then he turned and left without another word.

As soon as he had gone they agreed they could not just stay cooped up here they had to make an attempt to escape somehow.

During the day Felix was able to watch their captors collecting in groups checking their weapons and taking a shift in what Felix supposed was a radio receiving hut. They would take it in turns to monitor this radio so it was manned at all times. On one occasion a message was received and they all left hurriedly leaving only the three sentries on guard.

The only time during the whole day there seemed to be the remotest chance of escaping was overnight as their captors were very fond of consuming large amounts of a drink that filled the camp with the smell of aniseed. This made them both rowdy, argumentative and then finally fall silent with the exception of the odd loud snore. Over the next day or so they tried to collect any sharp or solid item they could to try to pierce the corrugated iron walls. They did manage to find some sharp stones but any attempt to pierce the metal made so much noise it was as if it was alarmed. They finally agreed that the only way out was through the palm plaited roof. As Belle was lighter she would sit on Felix's shoulders as she slowly made an opening in the corner of the roof at the opposite end to the door. Every attempt was made to try to conceal the hole but it would not have passed close inspection but their captors seemed uninterested in what they did.

CHAPTER 6

The next night they waited for the usual bun fight to commence, there was the usual clamour and noise and they started to get ready to make their escape. They waited for the din to subside to nothing but rasping snoring bouts and they made their move.

Although it seemed the wrong way round Belle had to lift Felix as high as she could to let him pull his way onto the pitch of the palm roof. Although the material had appeared tough and resilient while they were trying to force their way through it, this was a different type of loading altogether. The whole roof swayed as Felix pulled himself up towards the apex, small fronds fell to the floor scraping down the corrugated walls, he stopped waited and listened. Nothing other than the continual snoring filled the night. Felix removed his belt made a hand loop and passed it into the hole to Belle. "Ready?" whispered Felix "As I will ever be "replied Belle. Felix pulled and Belle slowly was pulled up onto the roof. As she was emerging through the hole Felix was dropping to the floor at the opposite end from the door. More pieces of the roof made their way to the floor but still nothing seemed to disturb the sentries. They both made their way to the ground and then to the edge of the clearing. There was still no noise so they moved silently out into the thick brush land.

After making a thirty minute trek away from the camp they stopped and tried to assess what their options were. Belle thought they could move inland as the pirate's base was obviously on the coast and her logic was the further away from them the better. Felix was of the opinion that if they hugged the coast there may be more chance of acquiring some kind of craft to make their escape. He expanded this logic with the fact that when the pirates realised they had lost their investment they would send out search parties and they would expect them to head inland. Eventually Belle agreed so they headed in what they thought was a westerly direction. The further they travelled the more the land began to get greener and softer underfoot. Eventually they found a place to take cover as the dawn approached. The land had become swamp like and the air damp with the musty smell of mangroves and rotting vegetation. Although they were both exhausted they made a makeshift den amongst the tangled mangroves.

Leaving Belle under cover Felix made his way to the rise ahead; he fancied he could smell salt on the air but disregarded this as untenable. He moved to the top of the rise and there he found he was looking down some hundred feet onto a natural inlet.

The entrance was narrow at the mouth but widened out to a harbour area large enough to accommodate a large number of small craft. The rock structure was such that the harbour area was not visible from the open sea and the overhanging rock also made it almost impossible to view from the air. Moored alongside these was an array of around fifty craft, sail cruisers. These included twenty Catamarans, three Trimarans and about a dozen Sunseekers and a similar amount of sail cruisers. This natural defence had been augmented by the addition of camouflage nets overhanging the docking areas. At the inner end of the inlet a large repair facility had been built into the rock face, this contained davit hoists and a fully fitted engineering workshop. Felix was amazed at the ingenuity and expertise of these Somalia pirates to be able to orchestrate such an operation. Especially having had some dealings with them they hardly seemed the most well organized bunch.

He watched as a mechanic removed the Perkins diesel engine from one of the outrigger boats, two things didn't seem right to Felix. Firstly, this was not an old reconditioned Perkins engine; this was the M210 26hp series that had only been made this year. Felix had drawn the plans for its fitting to two new naval Royal Naval Admirals landing barges. The other was the mechanic was wearing Royal Navy beetle crushers and the sound echoing softly off the water was the whistled strains of *"I am Sailing"*.

Felix was dumfounded. His own job meant he spent a lot of his time in Naval establishments around Britain and everything about this operation appeared, at first glance, to follow the same layout. Apart from the whistling matelot the small snippets of conversation he was able to pick up were all in English. There was a Parker crane hoist, used to remove medium sized craft out of the water, and again this was this year's specification.

He had to get back to Belle so he did not have time to watch any more but something was not quite as it seemed here he thought.

CHAPTER 7

F elix was suddenly awoken from his reminiscences as an alarm sounded on the automatic pilot navigational system it had detected an obstacle he leapt up and raced up the companionway and looked out into the black night. The wind seemed to have temporarily abated but the rain was still incessant. He looked at the screen which showed an obstruction dead ahead at around two hundred metres. He took the helm and followed the directions that the pilot had calculated and took her three points to port. He then activated the two high power halogen floodlights mounted each side of the wheel house. Then suddenly Felix saw the sea foaming around the base of several rocky outcrops that the ebbing tide had uncovered off Holkham Bay. He checked the screen again to ensure he was now in the clear.

He returned to the cabin and rechecked his charts, although the Neil Martin was sea worthy; she was only thirty feet, so he had to keep her relatively close to the coast. This meant he had to be aware of the sandbanks and the rocky out crops the Norfolk coastline is renowned for.

Felix had decided to make for the charmingly named Wells next the Sea, it was about eight miles, the last mile being up a coastal channel. In fact Wells were not next to the sea which made navigating the channel on an ebb tide a difficult operation. The whole of the Norfolk and Suffolk coast was continually being silted up by the fierce tides of the North Sea, this made even quite wide and deep channels lose draught clearance quickly. He took the Lincolnshire Belle into the tidal channel. Even with the ebbing tide he hoped to be berthed in the harbour in about an hour.

"One day" he thought *"this had to end"* but he had made a promise to Belle and to her his word would always be his bond.

Felix arrived at Wells quay at around 8pm, moored up, and signed the mooring log at the very ornate harbour office set adjacent to the quay. He then walked up Staithe Street and went into The Globe Inn. He had a pint of Bishops Finger and a double Jameson with a dash of water. The food menu was comprehensive and he feasted on a Cromer Crab dish, and at nine pm he wended his way back to the Lincolnshire Belle.

He made a couple of phone calls and hired a large estate car from a hire car company on the high street using his credit card on the internet.

He then settled his self-down with a bottle of 15 year old Jameson Special Reserve. Although the rain was still hammering on the cockpit roof the wind had now been replaced by rolling thunder and flashes of sheet lightening, which gave sudden flashes of ghostly white light across the nearly deserted Wells quay. At least the sea was calm and only a slight swell gently rocked the Lincolnshire Belle.

As the Jameson mellowed his mood Felix's mind drifted back to the inlet harbour he discovered near Baraawe. Just what had he discovered?. Was this the criminal fraternity funding and managing a lucrative business in a country where the government has no control? Was the profit in the ransoms' received from the hostage's relatives or in the resale of the luxury vessels that were captured with the victims?

Felix checked the internet for information on piracy in Somalia. The facts were astonishing. Since 2005 when the government lost control of the country, the rise in piracy has rocketed. The cost, if you include the ransom money paid, the loss of valuable vessels and their cargoes is around seven billion dollars per year. This does not include the insurance companies who have trebled the cost of cover for all craft that sail the Indian Ocean. The more Felix read the more he saw opportunities for international criminals to gain profit in so many ways, not just ransom, not just resale of the vessels, maritime insurance was another huge money earner. Finally if shipping companies would not use the Indian Ocean to deliver or collect cargo, due to the pirates, this left the field open for the same criminals to claim this highly priced service, a winner in so many ways. There was some suggestion that the Somalia government was somehow involved with the pirates but having seen the effectiveness of their attempted control of the country this was not a viable option.

He tried to recall all the details he saw the first time he came across the harbour but the overwhelming impression was that of a very professionally run operation and not that of a bunch of rag tag pirates.

CHAPTER 8

His mind ran back to his first discovery and how he returned to find Belle to let her know what he had seen. She was very pale and was sweating profusely. The humidity was very high and he thought she was starting to dehydrate. He knew he had to do something and do something quickly so he laid her back down covered her with any plant leaves he could find and went off in search of water. He knew there must be water available down in the harbour, so he followed the bay around till he reached the most inland point above the maintenance workshop.

He slowly worked his way down the steeply sloped side that was fortunately well covered in shrubs and trees until he reached the bottom twenty feet or so. At this point the rock took over and the grey and reddish slate like rock gave no hint of cover.

Felix swore under his breath, the harbour was alive with armed men either patrolling the mooring areas or carrying out works on a variety of craft. Just as he was about to admit defeat about accessing the area from here, a large claxon hooter sounded and the already highly active personnel became almost frenetic.

Entering through the narrow enhance slowly came a luxury Mediterranean Cruiser, she was over fifty feet long and her sleek white superstructure included a helicopter landing pad at the stern. The personnel had now lined up at the quayside to welcome the visiting dignitary. As he stared at the stern of the luxurious yacht he noticed that furled up on the stern flagpole was the Union Jack and that although she was registered in Honduras the name *He Who Dares* was quite a revelation. While the white suited, white hatted man and two other white clad VIP's were making his appearance on deck.

Felix knew this was the moment for his dash across the open rock. As he ran he kept his eyes on the figure clad in white and thought for a second he recognized the face but then dismissed it as impossible. He ran hard and low and slipped quietly into the water in the shadow of the repair area.

The greeting ceremony was now starting to decrease with the white suited supremo, and his guests, being escorted to a villa which was built into the bank and completely covered by undergrowth. Only at sea level could it be clearly seen. Felix knew his first priority was to get Belle some water.

As he was moving slowly into the repair shed he saw Vida Nova moored on the nearside jetty. He slipped quietly alongside and after a look down the jetty slipped noiselessly over the bow sheet.

He went straight to the rear lower cabin where he collected four flat polythene plasma bags. He then went to the forward hold where the water tanks were and he slowly filled all four bags which he tied around his waist through the loops on the bag. He filled his pockets with the gel additives that can be a substitute for food when you cannot hold solid food down during severe storms at sea.

He looked out from the base of the jetty to survey the scene and at that moment the slatted wood above him rattled as two mechanics had disembarked from catamaran moored on the other side of the jetty.

Felix heard them discussing the yacht.

"This cat is going to be renamed, remarked and new sails are arriving tomorrow, she will be worth around £350.000 on the open market."

"Money for old rope" his colleague laughed.

"What about the sailing yacht?" he went on looking at Vida Nova.

"She can wait, she's not worth more than £40,000."

"We will be taking the Sunseeker and the cat down to Aden tonight, so I will meet you here at 22.00 hours".

"We will tow the yacht with us and can use her to sail back."

"Good Idea" agreed the other man.

"It will take me back to my training days at Devonport" said the first ex matelot.

"I knew there was something about you I didn't like, I was trained at Pompey."

"Someone had to be "sneered his companion.

With that they walked off laughing towards the workshop.

Felix looked out again and there was a lot of movement on the far side of the inlet but this side was very quiet. Felix swam silently for the shoreline. He reached it with ease in no time and lay in the water's edge as he waited for his moment.

He had to wait some thirty minutes as two guards stationed almost directly opposite him stopped for a chat and a cigarette. Eventually they moved on and Felix ran for cover for all he was worth. He was slightly hampered by the water belt but he made the cover with no alarm being raised.

He clambered up the bank and after about forty five minutes he got back to find Belle.

CHAPTER 9

S he was still where Felix had laid her but she was even paler than when he had left her. The slight trembling and the cold perspiration did not bode well.

Felix lifted her gently and let her sip slowly from the water in the plasma bag; several times he had to stop her gulping the water too quickly. Slowly she seemed to be more alert but he let her lay back down to rest to conserve her depleted energy levels.

They stayed under cover during the rest of the day and the high humidity and thirty degree temperature made it sticky and very uncomfortable. He managed to get Belle to eat some of the high energy gel as well as sipping water over the whole day.

They were disturbed a couple of times during the day by the sound of footsteps and voices but they could not tell how far away they were. There was no sighting of anything other than a long green lizard that joined them in the mid-morning and rested with them all day.

As the light fell Belle was feeling much better almost back to her old self, she listened avidly to his description of what had happened in the harbour. Felix explained his plan for their escape to her, she felt it was feasible if not fool proof.

After taking on board some more gel and topping up their fluid levels and waving goodbye to their new found amphibian friend, they made their way to the edge of the inlet to survey the scene.

The light was failing quickly as it does on the sub-continent and they were able to make out figures moving around on the moorings and the jetties. The lights were on in the repair area and three craft were still moored there, the catamaran a Sunseeker and Vida Nova, which lay moored to the stern of the Sunseeker.

As the evening gloom descended hooded lights appeared which threw light downwards but avoided any tell-tale light glow on the dark skyline.

They worked their way slowly and silently down the steeply banked face of the inlet keeping under cover of the trees and shrubs. Felix followed his previous route and they arrived at the twenty foot danger zone and laid still.

The lights spread an opaque haze that shimmered on the water and caused a miniature light show on the lower levels of the surrounding banks.

They waited their time until there was a shout from the villa as the heads turned towards the source of the cry they darted across the open space and slid into the water of the bay. As they watched the guards stationed opposite burst into laughter as a man dressed in a chef's uniform ran and put his hand into the water. "You need to be more careful Domingo" the place for hot soup is in the bowl"

Felix and Belle slowly made their way to the repair area keeping just above the water level and hid alongside the jetty. There were two boiler suit clad workers on the deck of the catamaran, and they were just rewinding the mainsail back into its weatherproof canvas housing.

"That's a fine job if I say so myself" said the first guy in a thick scouse accent.

"You would though wouldn't you" growled a harsh Glaswegian voice.

"Let's get back to the bar for a drink" he continued.

They both left to find aforementioned bar.

Felix and Belle slid aboard Vida Nova and crept into the rear cabin where they found a comfortable hiding spot in the sailing store cupboard. Felix also found the Very pistol and the flares.

While Belle researched the charts, Felix made his way to the outboard engine ports and checked over the two Kawasaki Outriders. They seemed in perfect order well-oiled and although he could not run them up he was able to prime both units and check the charge on the electric starter unit.

These can be started manually, but electric starters are quicker and avoid the possibility of flooding, a real risk with outboards.

He then checked the sheets and released the locking mechanism so they could be run up as and when required. He was careful to ensure the ratchet was locked on the mainsail.

He finally checked the fuel tank and found it was nearly full. This had obviously been replenished by the two marine mechanics he had seen earlier.

Felix slipped over the side and slipped aboard the Sunseeker he made his way to the engine room and spent some time cutting nearly all the way through the electronic injection feed cables. These would be okay until the demand and the temperature increased and then they would shut down to protect the main engine.

He then visited the cat and disconnected the main rotor arm drives from the two Honda outboards. He returned to join Belle who was studying the charts by the light of a pencil light torch she found on the chart desk.

She had plotted a course that would take them to Mombasa in Kenya although this was some two hundred miles away.

"Well" said Felix "nothing to do but wait now"

CHAPTER 10

"Was there any food left on board?" asked Belle.

"I will have a look in the galley" Felix said,

He hurried away and returned with two tins of corned beef and a tin of creamed rice and of course a tin opener. He also found two bottles of flavoured water. They sat and ate ravenously they hadn't realised how hungry and thirsty they were.

They had to wait another hour before there was any movement on the jetty and then the two mechanics arrived and one boarded the Vida Nova checked the tow rope was securely fastened to the catamaran and hopped aboard the Sunseeker.

The huge engines of the Sunseeker shuddered into life and after clearing his departure on his radio he edged the two point five million dollar motor cruiser out into the harbour.

His colleague was in charge of the tow ropes as the cat and eventually the Vida Nova started to move away from the repair jetty. He spent his time with a fender pole ensuring the vessels stayed clear of the jetty. Once they were clear and moved out into the harbour the vessels began to straighten.

The Sunseeker made for the narrow entrance very slowly and although the tide level varied only a foot or two there was a lot of money on the move and any damage would not be received well.

Vida Nova was the last of the three craft to clear the entrance and as soon as they had open sea ahead the Sunseeker engines started to increase in power and the two tow vessels started to make headway.

From Felix and Belle's perspective being towed was a nightmare; the tiller was following rather than leading the motion of the yacht. These made her roll and pitch and at times almost skate on the surface of the water.

Felix made his way to the outboards and set them in run mode. He also unfurled the main sheet. Slowly the Sunseeker increased its speed to about twenty knots and running without navigation lights only the night pilot system could see in the dark.

They stayed aft and to the starboard side so out of sight of the other two craft, even though they were just black looming shapes.

Suddenly the roar of the Sunseekers engines changed to a stuttering misfiring and finally to silence.

Felix gunned the starters on the outboards while Belle cut the towing ropes. The main sheet was rolled out as the outboards burst into life Felix turned her about and opened up the two motors to full power they surged away in the opposite direction from the other two craft.

With Belle he hoisted the main sail and the foresail to get the maximum distance in the minimum time and they picked a fair wind aided by the high humidity on land.

They knew that the Sunseeker still had a radio and were able to call for back up so Felix went to the radio room and sent a Mayday call to the Kenyan Navy call sign.

He knew this was a gamble as his call may be picked up on the radio control centre which he guessed was housed in the villa. The advantage they had was they were running without navigation lights and in the pitch black they could sail straight by them unless they had night tracking on all their vessels.

As they sailed on in almost pitch darkness they found time to sit at the helm together.

"I am so sorry Felix" she said hugging his arm.

"What have you got to be sorry about" he asked smiling and then realising she could not see his face.

"I wanted to visit Nairobi and if we hadn't we wouldn't be in the trouble we are now" she said hugging his waist.

"If we use your thought process it was my fault for asking you to marry me" he laughed loudly.

"Then we would not be on honeymoon so therefore we would not be where we are now." he finished smugly.

She punched his arm hard and said.

"You know what I mean" she said now more mad than tearful.

"We agreed to make this our journey to visit places we hadn't seen" he continued.

"But I was the one who chose Nairobi" she persisted.

"No darling we chose Nairobi."

He left the wheel and took her in his arms.

"My place is with you wherever we go" he said kissing her passionately.

"Well you certainly know how to show a girl a good time" she said mockingly.

He pulled her towards him again "Let me see if I can set the pilot as I show you a good time again" he smirked.

"You are a scoundrel sir" she said dramatically.

He put on his best villains voice and as they slipped onto the cabin floor.

"Let the deflowering commence."

CHAPTER 11

F elix was suddenly brought back from his reminiscences as he was aware the Lincolnshire Belle was starting to roll as the onrushing incoming tide started to fill the mile long inlet of Wells harbour. As the banking was only slight the water could be seen visibly flowing and rising at an alarming rate. Felix quickly checked the clock it was six am so he put together his belongings on his two wheel trolley and made his way to the harbour masters office. He arranged for the Neil Watson to be moored at the fisherman's jetty on the other part of the harbour.

He moved swiftly up to the top of Straithe Street and into the hotel entrance of The Globe Hotel. The morning clerk gave him the keys and documents to his hire vehicle. He found the car in the hotel car park it was a two litre Renault Espace. He fitted his luggage into the rear seat area and checked the fuel gauge; it was full as he had agreed.

He pulled out of the car park and headed on coast the road to Cromer and then on the A140 to Norwich. The roads were incredibly quiet and he was able to make good time, even though Norfolk is the only county in Britain without a motorway.

Back at Wells Next the Sea, the incoming tide now had enough draught for a small motor patrol boat to surge into the harbour and moor at the jetty. The uniformed crew visited the harbourmasters office enquiring about any recent arrivals and departures.

This lead the crew to the Neil Watson moored at the fisherman's jetty. After a brief inspection the Captain radioed his base and reported what he had discovered. He then walked up the High Street to try to trace any possible clues to the fugitive's on-going journey.

Felix was on the outskirts of Norwich at just after eight am and he headed on the A11 towards the south. He planned to follow this till it reached the M11, and then follow this to the infamous London orbital the M25. Once on the outskirts of London he would go west on the M4 to Bristol and then south on the M5 to Exeter. He estimated the journey time at around four to five hours, dependant on the traffic and he hoped to reach his destination by early evening.

His mind went back to his hurried departure from the Lincolnshire Belle he had remembered to wipe all the fingerprints from all relevant surfaces, he had removed any personal belongings, he had his grey wig and his short grey beard he had worn on his visit to Wells and finally he had all his armoury broken down and packed in his incredibly heavy two wheel trolley.

He knew they would come on the tide as they would to all of the few navigable harbours on the Norfolk coast and that Wells was the first on the list. They had no idea what type of vessel they were looking for, but other than one that would be at home in this type of coastal waters; the Lincolnshire Belle fitted the bill perfectly.

The ownership of the Lincoln Belle was tied up in leasehold agreements with several offshore holding companies in Norway who specialised in hire contracts. So to trace its present owner would be a logistical nightmare.

On any other occasion he and Belle would have loved their stop at Wells and they would have meandered their way round the charming village while checking the quaint little shops and art galleries. Even more they would have enjoyed a long walk on the salt marshes on the estuary.

With their Nikon 50X zoom lens camera they would have been able to photograph the vast range of sea birds that flock to the area at low tide.

Such a short time had made such a large change in their lives he thought. It is amazing how a catalogue of extreme circumstances can cause your whole life to change your priorities. Things that had once seemed critically important now paled into insignificance.

It had caused Felix to re-evaluate his very existence and to focus his whole being into one purpose, saving Belle.

As he drove on he wondered how it would all end, he had had to grow up rapidly in the last eight months, gone was the devil may care attitude of the twenty five year old draughtsman. This had been replaced by a totally focussed individual. He had been taught how to train his already fit six foot frame to use weapons and to increase his fitness and endurance.

He knew if he was ever to see Belle again he would have to push himself to the limit and pit himself against a well-trained team of professionals.

CHAPTER 12

As he drove on he recalled the escape attempt on Vida Nova and how they sailed under sail and power for the next eight hours without seeing any sign of any pursuers. Felix estimated they had travelled around ninety miles and he knew they were eminently catchable, once the big engine sea cruisers were deployed. They checked the radio but there was no reply from the Kenyan Coastguard. As dawn started to break the natural phenomena took place and the wind picked up as it always seems to do in tropical climates and Vida Nova added another five knots to their speed. Belle was given the role of stern watcher with a pair of marine binoculars and as the light grew it was not long before she saw a dot on the horizon. At first, it was hard to distinguish, but soon took the shape of a fast moving vessel that sped towards them.

Slowly over the next two hours the speck on the horizon became larger until they could make out the shape of a motor cruiser that Felix assessed as traveling at around thirty five knots. Working on this principle it would be about another three hours before it would catch them up. He retried the Kenyan Navy on the radio but again with no reply.

They tried to eke the last ounce of speed from Vida Nova turning her into the wind to try to maximise the wind on the mainsail, this gave them another two knots. He also checked the two outboards that had been running now continually for eight hours, one was starting to overheat and Felix had to shut it down while he cleaned the air and the fuel filters. This reduced their speed by about five knots so the overall result was they were losing even more time to the following cruiser. As they were already running light there was nothing on board that could be jettisoned to increase their speed. He also knew the other outboard would also require shutting down once the first one had been overhauled. Things were not looking good and it seemed only a matter of time before they were re-captured.

After another two hours the pursuing cruiser could be plainly seen and the huge white bow wave showed she was still running flat out, Felix could even see crew members moving rapidly around the bow area but he could not see exactly what they were doing.

He returned the second now refurbished outboard and fired it into life and opened up the throttle, in an almost futile gesture, as the extra speed gained would make no difference on the vast distance of sea between them and Mombasa.

At last after another ninety minutes the cruiser was now only some three hundred metres away and was plotting a course to circle around them on the port side and come around to face them. Felix was surprised they did not just pull alongside and board them. It took another thirty minutes before the cruiser was in position and then their tactic became clear as the frantic activity on the bow area was the fitting of four inch machine gun and this was trained on Belle and Felix.

They then heard a voice via a loud hailer

"Heave too or you will both die".

"Well" said Felix as he looked at Belle "looks as though we are prisoners again".

At that moment there was a loud hissing sound as an armour plated shell landed about twenty feet to port of the cruiser, before they had time to react another shell landed only six foot away from the stern. The cruiser suddenly burst into life and with fully open throttles shot past Felix and Belle and headed off on the direction from which they had come.

As Felix and Belle looked out onto the starboard bow they saw a Royal Kenyan Navy Patrol boat cutting through the water like Thunderchild from the War of the Worlds story by HG Wells. The Patrol Boat hunted the cruiser down within minutes and the crew had no intention of putting up any resistance. In fact their first act was to dismantle and then throw the machine gun into the Indian Ocean. Felix and Belle watched as they were boarded and then taken aboard the Patrol Boat for interrogation. Four members of the Navy crew stayed aboard the cruiser to sail her back to the nearest safe port.

Felix and Belle were boarded by a small party from the Patrol Boat led by Lieutenant Wambui to whom they explained their story. He was impressed by the ingenuity of their escape and how far they had managed to get away from their captors. He was very interested about the harbour but even more interested in the VIP visitors.

Felix never mentioned that he thought he may recognized the VIP as he was sure he must have been mistaken.

They had to reluctantly leave Vida Nova with the two crew members on board who would sail her back to Mombasa. Felix and Belle boarded the Patrol Boat and enjoyed a good meal and a much needed shower and a borrowed change of clothes.

They arrived in Mombasa at around six pm on May 12 2009 and were taken to the Naval Intelligence Unit in the barracks. Here they were questioned by two officers and following this they were invited to dine with the Commanding Officer Admiral Nelson Murithi. He had sent all of the intelligence collated to the Kenyan Navy's Headquarters also in Mombasa; they would take the decision as to whether any direct action could be taken on Somalia soil.

The crew of the Sunseeker were to be taken to Nairobi where they would appear in court.

They left the Admiral after about two hours and were shown to a very comfortable room where they slept for ten hours without stirring. They arose, and after a hearty breakfast, they were shown to the Vida Nova to check her over. They were warned they may be called as witnesses in the case of the attempted Piracy and that they may need to return to Kenya.

CHAPTER 13

They asked for an escort from the Kenyan Navy to the Gulf of Aden as they headed for the Suez Canal on their homeward voyage. This they did and they had a long but eventless journey back across the Indian Ocean. When they reached the Gulf of Aden an Indian Royal Navy Patrol Cutter escorted them to the Suez Canal via a soothing voyage through the Red Sea.

They sailed the canal and were astounded at the varying size of craft they passed from large tankers and cargo ships to small dhows and outrigger canoes. Although the surroundings had no great landscape views to offer they could not help but be amazed by the engineering feat in building this waterway through this desolate and arid land. They eventually reached Port Fuad at the mouth of the Mediterranean Sea on May 27 2009 and the inactive and sluggish water of the Suez Canal and the highly salted tide free Red Sea were replaced by the permanently wind driven Mediterranean. These last few weeks had recharged Felix and Belles batteries and they were starting to enjoy the feel of the sea and the smell of the salt again. They stopped at Alexandria to take on fresh supplies, they marvelled at the marketplace and fell about laughing as they pretended to barter like a character from Monty Pythons "The Life of Brian" over a gourd. It was hot and dusty and they were glad to re-board Vida Nova where the air was cleaner and cooler.

Felix was listening to the BBC World service when the story of an accident on the main road to Nairobi was broadcast. Two vehicles, a fuel tanker and a prison security wagon, collided on the Menaga Bridge and both vehicles fell three hundred feet into the ravine below. According to Police statements there were no survivors

"No loose ends you mean" said Felix.

Following this news Felix and Belle became super cautious never going anywhere unarmed, and yet they were nearly caught by the proverbial sucker punch.

They ordered supplies for their next leg of the voyage and they were delivered to the quayside by the local ships chandler. As the goods were being stowed aboard Felix noted that there were more water containers than they had ordered so he spoke to the delivery driver.

"Sorry sir" he said "I only deliver the items and the amount tallies with my dispatch note".

All the items with the exception of the water containers were loaded aboard and Felix was standing beside the filtered tanks on the quay. He studied the nearest containers all had the seal intact so he moved one container aside and checked another he again checked the seal but this had been tampered with and he quickly inspected the barrel closely.

He smelt the fuel immediately and then saw the fuse wire attached, he called to Belle as the delivery guy returned to the quay. The driver took a Glock 15 automatic pistol from his pocket and opened fire. Felix nearly took cover behind the tanks, a suicidal move as they were an inferno waiting to be ignited, just then he saw Belle dive off the other side of Vida Nova into the harbour "*good girl*" he thought.

Felix opened fire roughly in the direction of the driver, who was racing back to his van, but the driver turned and aimed a barrage of shells at the barrels. One of the shots made contact and the barrels exploded throwing Felix straight off the other side of the quay he flew above a small fishing boat and hit the water with such force that all the wind was taken out of him. Due to the speed of his entrance into the water he took in a large amount of heavily tainted sea water in through his mouth and nose. He drifted along the shallow harbour bed before slowly ascending under the crisscross timbers of the main jetty. Slowly he regained his senses after bouts of retching and dizziness. He managed to climb the jetty ladder but the place was alive with people all frantically trying to establish what had happened.

He eventually, he reached the jetty where they had been moored there was no sign of any barrels, only a large hole in the jetty. The delivery van, or at least a black burnt shell of one, was twenty feet up the jetty and Vida Nova was drifting some fifteen feet off the jetty. *"Belle must have untied her before she jumped"* thought Felix.

He searched the water for Belle but there was no sign of her. He spotted a uniformed officer from the harbourmasters office.

"Did anyone see what happened to my wife?" he asked.

"She was one of the lucky ones. Someone picked her up in a launch."

"Do you know where they took her?" said Felix.

"No they went towards the harbour mouth" replied the officer.

Belle was snatched on 17 June 2009.

They managed to find another berth for Vida Nova and a quick inventory showed only superficial damage she would be ready for sea in a few days.

The following day he was visited by a smartly dressed man who spoke with a clipped northern accent. He was around six foot three inches tall but only weighed around a hundred and thirty pounds.

"Look upon me as a fortune teller" he said.

"You are going to disappear without trace and if you do your wife will stay alive" he went on.

"But if you contact anyone she will die."

"Do you understand me?" he snarled.

"Yes" Felix replied.

"Good" he said "Otherwise the next time we meet not only will I have killed her but I will kill you."

"No" said Felix "if you touch a hair on her head I will promise I will kill you."

The fortune teller smiled walked towards Felix and said.

"Don't try to play with the professionals laddie" he said then strolled casually down the gangplank and walked up the jetty without looking back.

Felix had calculated the whole thing had taken about three minutes.

He could not believe that they had kidnapped Belle so as to ensure his silence over what, or more importantly who they think he had seen at the pirate's cove.

They obviously tried to kill them both at the dockside and he assumed the water tanks were meant to ignite while they were at sea. If they could access him that easily why did they not just kill him and there would be no need to take Belle hostage. There must be some reason why they did not want another death reported at present.

All Felix knew was that he had to get Belle back and he had to do it quickly in case they felt her usefulness was at an end.

He had to let Belles family know what had happened and he had to try to stop her dad from flying out to arrange a search party. He promised to keep them informed of any developments as they happened.

On that day Felix Barnard began his metamorphosis from easy going young man with a penchant for sailing to a dedicated focused individual who had only one aim in his life.

He sailed to Cyprus and moored at Paphos in the old harbour where he was told he could acquire illegal weapons easily. It took only two days to find the contacts but to fund these weapons he had to sell his beloved Vida Nova but he had no time for sentiment it was a way to an end as far as he was concerned. He bought a small Seat van in Paphos and this he loaded with his entire recently acquired arsenal.

The drive across Greece and then onto France was slow and arduous but the distance was covered and eventually Felix found himself at Le Harve waiting for the ferry to Dover. He had made specific hiding places for all his weapons prior to the start of this journey and now their effectiveness would be put to the test. He boarded the eleven forty five pm ferry and parked in his allotted space. He left the vehicle found himself a comfortable chair and settled down for the night

The ferry arrived at six am at 31 June 2009 and slowly the disembarkation took place he drove his Seat to the checkpoint where a young Customs and Excise officer looked over in and under his vehicle. Just as he was about to drive off another Officer approached and approached Felix directly.

"Mr Barnard" he asked looking at a list on his clipboard.

"Can we have a word with you sir please?" Drive your car over to the side of the office if you would ".

Felix thought about flooring the Seat but knew he had nowhere to run so did as he was instructed. He was escorted inside where a tall grey haired immaculately dressed man in a Crombie coat and old school tie.

"Good morning Mr Barnard welcome to England" he said extending his hand.

"I have had a communication from one of our team regarding two incidents, one in the Indian Ocean and one in Alexandria harbour."

Felix started and then tried to remain calm but it was too late.

"We know they have kidnapped your wife Felix, may I call you Felix? It seems we are on the same side".

Remembering the threat from the gunman he was unsure what to do so he replied.

"I have no idea what you are talking about my wife is on holiday in Africa" he said with what he thought was conviction.

"This is hard fact Felix I do not deal in any other currency" replied the Crombie," I can even tell you the time exactly the kidnap took place" he went on, "we have the incident on film if you would like to watch"

Felix made a decision. "I have been told she will be killed if I talk to the authorities"

"Just as well you are dealing with us then as we do not exist" he went on quietly.

"I can deal with these people myself" Felix said.

"Not without our help you can't" he replied.

"Look Felix let me introduce myself I am Commander Hutchins from Military Intelligence" I am a member of the International Crime team and we are aware of the situation in Somalia".

"You and your wife stumbled across an important clue when you found one of their harbours"

"But" he added "a far bigger clue was the owner of the He Who Dares who would appear to be a major player".

"But I never saw his face, feeling a sudden pang of guilt "answered Felix,

"No, but does he know that. He does know you are able to give a detailed description of his yacht" Hutchins went on.

"What do you want me to do?" asked Felix.

"I want you to disappear while we search for your wife" replied Hutchins.

"And when you find her?" Felix asked.

"Then you can go and rescue her" replied Hutchins.

But I have no idea how to do that" said Felix "Then we will have to teach you" replied Hutchins "One thing I don't understand" said Felix "Why not just kill us both when they had the chance?"

"They tried" replied Hutchins" you and your wife were meant to be killed in an explosion at sea, or even a shot on the quayside" he went on" but the botched attempt made them think again, also another attempt on the lives of two British nationals would have caused quite an international incident, especially after your recent visit to the Kenyan Navy at Mombasa."

"This way you just disappear quietly" continued Hutchins "Your silence is guaranteed by them having Belle as a hostage."

"But what's the chances they will they keep her alive?" asked Felix.

"All the time you are alive she is safe" said Hutchins

"So learn to stay one step ahead" continued Hutchins.

"I have promised her father I will keep him informed of any developments" said Felix.

Hutchins smiled gently "We will ensure Mr Worthington is aware of what is happening" he said patting Felix on the shoulder.

"Well off you go, you are going to school for a while".

Hutchins left and without any further ado Felix was taken to a nearby sport fields where a Sea King helicopter was waiting to take him to Hereford where his training started the next day at 5am.

For six weeks he was taught, bullied, encouraged, and exercised unlike anything he had ever known. Although he was quite fit he found the standards required to appease the ever more demanding NCO's really pushed him to the limits of his capabilities.

This training was not just physical but mental attitude and learning to rely on instinct and act without hesitation. "Hesitation kills" was the watchword of one Warrant Officer "Your instinct is your best friend so follow it blindly" he remarked as he walked past Felix's perfectly camouflaged hiding place just prior to hitting him on the head with his rifle butt.

He was taught to use explosives and how to prime and time set charges.

He learnt to use a vast array of weapons and at the end of his training even his platoon Sergeant, a hard-bitten Glaswegian enthused "You'll do."

He completed his training on August 8 2009. Although he was not able to carry out the full training he was given a broad based selection of the skills he needed to stay alive.

The plan was made to find a hideaway that could be defended against organised attack and the Lincolnshire Fens were selected due to their very difficult terrain and their isolated position.

Felix was given access to the funds required via a credit card and he also had funds in cash for items that were hard to hide on a purchasing log sheet.

He was also kitted out with the latest equipment and weaponry available and started the long process of building a fortress with a means of escape in case it all went wrong.

He moved into the windmill on 10 August 2009. It was the loneliest time he had ever known.

CHAPTER 14

Felix jumped as his mobile phone rang. He was only five miles from the M25 and he read the text message on his screen.

"Car traced via internet expect full scale search".

Felix sighed "I wondered how long it will be?"

He was on the westbound carriageway of the M25 heading for Newbury when he heard the small monoplane fly low and slowly over the carriageways.

"Could be just any traffic reporter" he thought as it flew right above him the glint of a pair of high powered binoculars caught in the pale late afternoon sun. The next accessory protruding from the cockpit did not fit so well with his theory of weathermen it was a full size sniper rifle and the pilot was turning full circle a half mile ahead so as to approach him head on.

Felix remembered his training; make the target as small and as elusive as possible. So he started snaking the Renault between the lanes, this action caused car horns to be sounded all around him and also people on all carriageways looked over to see what had happened. The plane held back on from its intended course as there were too many eyes watching.

He had to get off the motorway where he was a sitting duck, so he saw Junction twenty six ahead that lead to Epping Forest so he sped off down the slip road. He turned left on the A121 and headed for the forest. The Cessna had by now turned and was flying in low again following the slip road. The A121 was a part tree covered road, but the spaces were wide enough to allow a marksman to easily pick off a moving target.

At the next bank of trees Felix pulled the Renault off the road and tucked it as tightly as he could against the tree trunks.

From the boot he took his Accuracy International 7.62mm sniper rifle and quickly loaded the clip.

As the plane approached at only ten feet above from the road Felix saw the first shell go straight through the windscreen and embed itself in the rear seat. Felix waited as the pilot looped back so they could have another shot but this time Felix was ready. He took careful aim, and remembering his training, squeezed the trigger gently. The pilots head jerked back and the sepia patch showed on the cockpit to the rear of his head. The Cessna Mustang flew straight into the trees on the opposite side of the road.

Despite his short, sharp training this was the first time he had killed a living target. The whole thing had an unreal feeling to it and he felt slightly detached from it. It was almost as if someone else had pulled the trigger. If he had had time to sit down and think about it may have been more traumatic but his first sense activated was that of self-preservation. He looked at the bullet hole in the windscreen and the back seat and he knew there would have been no remorse had this bullet killed him. This somehow comforted him and drove him on to make good his escape.

Felix drove off towards London parked the Renault in the Autopoint Renault dealership car park at Forest Road Walthamstow. He then walked to Hoe Street to catch the tube to Waterloo, where he boarded the 14:45 to Exeter.

While he sat on the tube he was mulling over in his mind how they traced his location so quickly. It was possible that if you looked at the map from Norwich that there were not many main roads that left Norfolk and maybe the M11 was the fastest way to cover the miles.

It was also possible that the Renault had a GPS tracking system fitted and if you had access to the hire companies system this maybe another possibility. Nevertheless, the location of the Renault by the Cessna was amazingly fast and Felix felt that he needed to be very careful who he trusted.

As instructed he sent a text in code saying *"Mother is okay but she had to be taken into a nursing home"*. On the long stretch between stations, somewhere between Guildford and Chichester, the phone made an unscheduled stop in the River Arun, just in case it contained a tracker device. He arrived at Exeter St David's station at five ten pm and by twenty to six pm he made his way to the nearest hotel. The Globe was opposite the station, he booked in for one night.

The long dark haired rather studiously dressed Professor Llewellyn was from Cardiff University and was in Exeter to have a meeting at Exeter University the following morning. When Felix first learned to role play he felt awkward and out of place but with experience he was now able to engage with other guests and this he found made people more accepting of you and less likely to remember you for the wrong reason.

Shy retiring people are always suspected of being up to no good so the more you interact the better you will be accepted. Felix also had improved his quality of disguise and again he had learned that less was more. If you overdo a disguise you make yourself look out of place and this is exactly the opposite of what you are trying to do.

He now also had total confidence in his adopted characters and was totally at ease being whoever he chose to be. He had spent three days with a master of disguise who could change his appearance merely by holding himself differently, speaking differently, walking differently so the actual disguise needed to be very little.

People will expect you to fall into certain preconceived categories and if you use these as your blueprint people will accept you readily. Felix was never told his mentors real name and due to his amazing control of accents Felix was never sure which one was his own, but when he left he gave Felix the best advice he could ever receive on wearing disguises "Believe you are who you are pretending to be" he said "if you cannot fool yourself you will never fool others".

After a leisurely meal of soup, sirloin steak with a Stilton sauce and an Irish coffee Felix, retired to his very comfortable room. From his backpack he took out a brand new mobile phone and loaded a newly bought SIM card and sent a new message *"Hire car needs clean up team to remove luggage Autopoint Walthamstow"* he sent the message then totally destroyed both phone and SIM card. One with a heavy duty ash tray and the other with a cigarette lighter.

He needed to have the depth charges removed from the Renault and the gun shot damage repaired before it was returned to the hire company.

He then went through the local Thompson Directory and found a budget hire company based at the railway station. Earlier he had contacted Roger Young Land Rover at Saltash and made an offer on a Defender 90 2.5 Td5 County and he agreed to call in the following day to sort out the details.

With that done Professor Llewellyn slept soundly until eight am when he went down for his full English breakfast. He paid for the hire car, a well-used Ford Focus, with cash and was on the road to Saltash by 9am.

He drove across Dartmoor past Moretonhampstead until he reached Yelverton. There he joined the A386 and turned right onto the A38 onto Saltash. He arrived at the Land Rover dealership at ten twenty five am and spent the next hour and a half sorting out the payment and the insurance details. Felix also bought a heavy duty tow rope and a set of extra grip tyre sleeves that can be fitted over the already heavily treaded off road tyres.

It was just after midday that Felix drove out onto the slip road and was straight back on the A38 and heading west. He stopped at a large retail store outside Lisekard stocking up with a comprehensive collection of food and household items. He then continued to Bodmin and then onto A389 to Wadebridge. Here he took B3314 to the tiny hamlet of St Minver.

Just before the village he turned left up a very steep lane which had been turned into a flowing stream as the ever persistent rain fell again. He followed the lane up the hill for the next twenty minutes until he was surrounded only by fields and the low hedges. He then turned into the yard of a farmhouse that was perched high on the top of the hill that had uninterrupted views inland and was only forty feet away from the sheer cliff face.

He unloaded the goods into the refurbished farmhouse and within thirty minutes he had managed to make up and light the fire in the living room, activate the central heating boiler and prime and fire up the four stroke generator in one of the outhouses.

Although it was only just after 4:30pm it was already dark and Felix went out to place some movement detectors down along the entrance lane and on the gates and finally on the external hedges of the yard. He had a set of Halogen movement activated floodlights fitted all around the farmhouse.

He parked the Land Rover in another outhouse set the alarm and set up his infra-red cameras to look out to all four sides of the building.

He pulled the steel shutters down on all the windows and walked down the lane to look back at the farmhouse, no light whatsoever showed from the building even on this pitch black night. Happy with what he saw Felix walked back to the building and secured the front door. He arrived at the farmhouse on the 11 December 2010.

He walked to the kitchen to prepare a gastronomic delicacy, but ended up with grated really strong cheddar cheese, baked beans, and two fried eggs on toast. He never realised just how tiring the day had been. After enjoying, this with the equivalent satisfaction of a gourmet meal, he treated himself to some Cornish ice cream as a dessert.

He sat with a coffee and a Jameson, some things cannot be replaced, in front of the blazing fire and tried to take stock of the situation. He studied his Jameson, as he held his lead crystal glass to the flames of the fire, and marvelled at the clear golden nectar. He wondered how his little lady was doing, was she still alive he had to believe she was.

Not for the first time over the last few days he doubted his own determination and ability to be able to do what was required of him. *"Maybe she's already dead"* he thought to himself, all this could be just a waste of time, and at that moment he felt that cold hand on his heart. His body inadvertently shuddered and he stared into flames of the fire. *"No she's not dead I would feel it if she was"* he pounded his fists on the fireplace. "I would know" he repeated loudly. He even managed a wry smile.

He knew he would be tested to the limit and he prayed he would be man enough to pass this test.

He heard his platoon Sergeant saying in that gruff Glaswegian voice "You'll do" "I bloody well will do"

"Where are you my baby" he cried out in despair.

CHAPTER 15

Belle was sitting on a stone bench in a Cotswold stone outbuilding that had two foot thick walls and only one tiny window that was built up in to the apex of the end wall. The building had obviously been used to raise livestock over the winter months and there were still tell-tale black and white feathers where last year's Christmas turkeys had been raised.

She had been taken from the water in Alexandria harbour onto a launch and then a motor cruiser moored outside Alexandria harbour. She noticed that she was named Mariner and registered in Honduras. As she was escorted aboard she also noticed there were at least a dozen crew members, maybe more, as she could only see those topsides. She was taken to a dingy storage room on the lower decks which was filled with ropes and canvas bags. She was roughly dragged to the cabin, the door was opened, and was thrown in by a swarthy looking sailor who she took to be Greek.

She never learned any clue as to what was going on. Various seaman brought food and water on a twice daily basis and some leered at her now torn and holed blouse. One even tried to grab her but she kicked out at his personal assets and he quickly retreated hissing and swearing. She was visited, on her penultimate day on the yacht, by a short but broadly built man dressed in a captain's uniform. He explained that as long as she carried out the instructions given to her she would not be harmed. He said she would be moved to a safe location and that if her husband acted sensibly, then in time she would be set free.

Belle watched the swarthy skinned man closely and although his manner was relaxed and calm she felt this was a man would do whatever he had to get the job done.

She was taken from this yacht to a wooden barn on a hot and humid shoreline. There was no way to see out of the barn, the sturdy wood panels had been over boarded to deny any light filtering in and any possible view out. The soil was red and sandy and she guessed they were somewhere in Sardinia or Corsica.

She could hear the sea continually and she guessed she was less than a mile from the coast. Here she was given a meal of fruit and maize and a mug of tepid water once a day. Despite her best efforts to escape by trying to dig the red soil from around the sturdy wooden planks all she succeeded in doing was make her fingers bleed and blacken all her nails.

This was Belles lowest ebb and she began to think that she would never leave this place. She had no idea how long she had been held captive, but her nails had become incredibly blackened and long, her hair, now matted and tangled, had grown way down onto her shoulders. It had to be several weeks she even tried to mark five bar gates on the wood but the wood was too dry and hard.

Apart from the looks of the guards on food duty and the muttered obscenities she was left pretty much to her own devices. Her two biggest issues were the tepid water causing continual stomach upsets and the total boredom and lack of any meaningful conversations. As the weeks passed she deteriorated physically and started to sleep for long periods of the day.

Then one day without warning the doors opened and two less than welcoming guards took her into the bright sunlight, which nearly blinded her. They took her to a shower cubicle obviously used to wash the salt water from bathers after swimming.

She stayed in the shower for nearly thirty minutes slowly luxuriating in the cold but clean water. She was then taken to a small lean to building where she was sat, at a rickety cane table, and was served a meal of spiced chicken and rice with a bottle of Perrier water.

She savoured the food as if it been produced in a three star Michelin restaurant and sat staring at the blue ocean. Unfortunately her stomach could not take the highly spiced food and this caused her to be unwell for the next day or so.

She was then visited by a more amenable guard who gave her some vitamin tablets and offered her more bottles of Perrier and a box of sugared almonds. "You need to get your strength up lady we are travelling again tomorrow" and with that he left, after giving her a pai of nail scissors, with which she was able to cut her now *Fu Man Chu* length finger and toe nails. She was supervised by the guard during this operation and when they were done to her satisfaction she was returned to her shed.

The following day she was taken back to the same yacht and was put back in the same storage room and her travelling began again but more importantly her confidence was starting to return. She had always been confident as a child, mostly due to the continual support she had received from her family, but this had been tempered by an inner humility which made her approachable to all. This had meant she had a wide range of friends from all levels of society. She could name the Admirals of both Lymington and Portsmouth Sailing clubs as personal friends and to counter this she was also a regular visitor to the Homeless units at Lyme Regis and Lymington.

When she first met Felix they had faced the trials and tribulations that learning to sail can bring and those experiences had built up a bond that had grown into love over the years. He was obviously the target of her captors but they had never asked her anything about what they knew or had seen.

The only reason she could come up with to explain this was that they already knew what they knew and what or who they had seen. Knowing Felix, he would put his heart and soul into avoiding being found and his resourcefulness would be essential in staying one step ahead. The following night she was taken ashore in a small launch, and although they covered her eyes, she was sure this was Swanage on the Dorset coast. She was put in the back of a covered van and driven for four or five hours overnight. She was then led into a stone outhouse that had a heater, electric light and a bed placed in the corner. There was also a stone bench and a chemical toilet. Compared to her last prison this was five star accommodation.

God speed Felix she prayed.

Commander Hutchins was sat at his desk in Whitehall looking at the last messages from Felix. The first was that he had been traced, secondly the loss of the Lincoln Belle at Wells. These were not unexpected but the tracing of the Renault so quickly only gave credence to his belief that there was mole in his team. He had dispatched a team to repair the Renault and remove the items from the Lincoln Belle. He did not blame Felix for only using a phone once as it made GPS tracing almost impossible. He also cleared the fourteen thousand pounds withdrawal from his personal credit card account that Felix had used. He knew he was in the West Country but it was best that they did not know exactly where. The tracing of Belle was going slightly better the GPS trace had tracked a motor cruiser leaving Alexandria at the time of the incident. At this point they lost the trail for three months when it was picked up leaving Sardinia. After this it was tracked to the West Coast at Swanage. Here unfortunately they had lost one of the three vehicles that had left the harbour together, the two they tailed ended up at Plymouth and Lands End. The records of a black Mercedes van were going through the PNC system while he waited. We are relying on you Felix mused Hutchins as he stared at his computer screen.

Felix awoke the following morning and carried out his security checks all was clear. He had a quick bacon and egg sandwich, a lesson he had learned, was always eat when you have the opportunity as you never know when you will have a chance again. The West Country bacon was thick cut, smoked and very tasty as were the three free range eggs.

He went to check the Land Rover and retrieved some more weapons from the floor plate cavity. One of the main difficulties of living on the run is finding things to pass the time meaningfully and not get obsessed with security.

Felix had become interested in birds and wildlife and used his high power binoculars to watch and record bird species. He had also learned to whittle wood and he had become an avid follower of outdoor survival techniques.

Today his mission was to scout a five mile radius of the farmhouse and plant tell-tales and remote sensors. He had already placed these sensors in the close proximity of the house and today it was the turn of the outer perimeter ring.

It was another average January day the rain fell in a fine drizzle that can soak you to the skin without any apparent rainfall. The wind came in gusts off the sea and the sky was several shades of dark grey and black.

Felix finally completed his tour of the house at around three pm and it was already getting dark. He went into the farmhouse relit the coal fire and activated the oil fired central heating.

He needed to dry off and get a meal on and have a nice hot bath.

By five o'clock he had managed all of these with the exception of the hot meal, but the oven was omitting a lovely aroma of a beef casserole, roast potatoes and fresh vegetables from the cold store.

He ate quickly and even opened a bottle of Cabernet Sauvignon as a special treat. The heating was on and the smokeless coal fire was burning bright. Even though it was smokeless fuel its chimney fumes were extracted into a duct connected to an inlet of an old tin mine. So with the shutters closed the place looked deserted.

He hoped to god he found Belle before they found him.

CHAPTER 16

Hutchins was driving through Sussex countryside when he got the news they had traced the black Mercedes van to the outskirts of a village called Moreton in the Marsh in the middle of the Cotswolds. The vehicle was found totally destroyed by fire in a disused farmyard about a mile from the village. His team were scouring satellite footage to see if the switch was recorded on the satellite sweep.

He pulled into the drive and stopped at the double gates of a large country house. He did not have to ring as the CCTV had already traced his approach for the last mile and were well aware of who he was. "Welcome sir" said a remote voice as the big gates smoothly swung open "Please drive to the library entrance" continued the disembodied voice. Hutchins knew where he was going as he had been here many times; his host was Sir Henry Waddington-Walker the Home Secretary and the minister responsible for state security.

He went through the normal security checks at the entrance to the building and was then shown into the very ornate library itself. This room and the rest of this glorious thirty room mansion had been restored slowly to its eighteenth century glory by the Walker family over the last fifty years.

"Hello Jim" said Sir Henry as he rose from the beautifully hand carved writing desk. "What is the latest on Barnard and his wife?"

"Well" replied Hutchins "We have traced her to the Cotswolds, after we eventually picked up her trail in Sardinia and we know Barnard is in the West Country."

"Do we know where exactly?" Asked Henry.

"No sir" Hutchins replied really glad he did not have to lie. "What do we know of the mystery man Barnard saw?" continued Henry

"Nothing sir" replied Hutchins "There is of course no craft registered with that name in Honduras or anywhere else" he continued "and Barnard was unable to give a description of the man himself."

Sir Henry tapped the desk gently and said "So why we are still involved in this Jim if there is no pot of gold for us at the end?"

Hutchins pondered before answering "Well sir, we are using Barnard as bait, if he flushes out the hit team, we will have a chance to interrogate actual members of the organisation".

It was Sir Henry's time to pause before continuing "I have known you a long time Jim, and I have read your reports on these well organised piracy incidents. You believe that someone within the British government is orchestrating this multi-million pound operation" he paused again "That is why you are playing your cards so close to your chest am I correct?"

"I cannot say that is correct sir, but it is a field of investigation I have not ruled out" replied Hutchins.

Sir Henry laughed out loud "Okay Jim in future only you and I will have access to the full information. Other teams will have access on a need to know basis"

"Thank you sir" smiled Hutchins.

"Go on off with you and good luck with your mole hunt".

Hutchins left the building and drove slowly home to his own quite substantial detached home in the stockbroker belt of Surbiton. A bit too glib was his assessment of the Home Secretary's response. *"He knows more than he is telling"* thought Hutchins.

Hutchins entered his front door and was greeted by Leona Hutchins, his wife of twenty four years. "Hello Jim" she said pecking him on the cheek. "I wasn't sure if you were coming home tonight. I will go and fix you something to eat."

"Sorry Lonny, I should have let you know" he said apologetically. "I am used to it by now" she laughed as she made her way to the kitchen. He watched her go and thought how the dickens had she stayed married to him for so long. He was out all hours had never had time to do normal things that families do and yet she was still there. When she came back to lay the table he wrapped his arms around her and gave her big kiss and a hug. Lonny smiled and said "And what was that for?"

"For putting up with me" he said "Not many would" he finished knowingly. She smiled at her absentee husband and said "I could have done a lot worse" and strode back into the kitchen to complete her culinary masterpiece.

Sir Henry was on the phone as soon as Hutchins left "Sorry to disturb you Prime Minister" "but we need to meet, something has come up".

CHAPTER 17

B elle was by now bored out of her mind. Apart from the three times a day opening of the lower door to pass through breakfast, lunch and what tasted like frozen meals for one in the evening, she was left totally alone. Following her time in the shed her treatment here was almost four star hotel standard. Being a geologist she recognized the Cotswold stone easily and she also knew it is nowhere near as hard as it looks. She managed to collect two knives and a spoon from her meals without anyone noticing, and she then started the long process of scraping away at the joins between the stones where the outhouse abutted up to another. After another week she could see daylight between the bottom stones.ed she remember her father's saying *"slowly slowly catchee monkey."*

Felix left the farmhouse early the following morning as he needed to collect a few essentials and suitably attired in his flat tweed cap, green wellingtons, waxed Berber jacket and green corduroy trousers, he left for a trip to Launceston. To complement the country attire, he chose the short grey beard and rimless glasses. The early morning fog was almost impenetrable at the top of the tor by the farmhouse and even worse as the road dipped down into St Minver, a deserted village this time of year, but a thriving holiday resort in the summer months. The drive to Launceston was slow but uneventful and Felix drove into the little market town and parked in the square. He walked to the local supermarket and stocked up on more tinned produce and long life milk and of course a fifteen year old Jameson. He then walked to the local gunsmith and bought some black cartridges for his double barrelled Remington shotgun. He called in to the general hardware store where he bought a sixty metre high tensile rope ladder and a twenty climbing hoops and the same number of tensioning straps. These are often used to get down to cattle or sheep that have strayed down the cliff areas and get stranded on ledges. Finally he went to the electrical store where he purchased four new mobile phones and four new SIM cards.

He loaded a new card in a new phone and called Hutchins. "Hello" said Hutchins not recognizing the number.

"I am at my new home Uncle" said Felix "That's good" replied Hutchins "are you happy with your neighbours?" he asked "So far so good" replied Felix." Have you been able to find my missing cat?" asked Felix, "Not yet but she was seen very recently" said Hutchins "We will find her soon" he added. "Any in-house help?" asked Felix "A very close friend" replied Hutchins. With that Felix who had been watching the clock during the call ended the call and crushed the phone and card. Hutchins smiled as the phone went dead this young man had become a professional by necessity.

Felix filled the Land Rover with fuel and also filled three jerry cans each containing five gallons as a stand by. He then slowly drove his way home even stopping for a Cornish pasty at a little roadside café. He was so impressed with the "oggies" that he bought a couple to take home. As he approached the farmhouse he began his usual checking procedure, checking tell tales and sensors and only when he was happy did he drive through the farmhouse gates. He had arranged to have 1,500 litres of propane gas delivered to the house prior to his arrival and paid for it as part of the lease on the property. He knew the next two months would be cold and snowfall was virtually guaranteed so his escape routes would be severely restricted.

After stowing the food and relighting the fire he made his way to the cliff face at the end of the sixty foot vegetable garden. Although the sky had taken on that light grey colour, that usually precedes snowfall, he looked over the cliff face. There were several grassy ledges recessed into the top ten feet of the cliff but after that the cliff face became sheer granite as it fell a 150 feet to the sea below. As the cliff face reached the sea there was a mass of huge granite rocks that seemed determined to repel the seas endless assault. Felix returned to the outbuilding that housed the workshop and returned with a hydraulic power gun and two stainless steel climbing hoops. He used the gun to fire a hardened steel tapered internal sleeve into the rock at the top of the cliff edge. He repeated this four times until he was able to fit the hoops into the four holes by driving them into the taper with a sledge hammer. Slight snow flurries were in the air but Felix continued and secured the sixty metre rope to the climbing hoops.

Once this was completed he threw the rope over the cliff face. He knew he had to secure the rope with extendable loops to keep it from moving wildly once his weight was on it. The first four brackets were easily fixed using his hydraulic gun but as he travelled further down it was too unstable to use this method of securing the rope. He managed to fix another four brackets by hand, using a climbing pick and a lump hammer but had to give up as the light was failing and the snow had now become faster and the flakes were the size of fifty pence pieces. He climbed to the top of the cliff face checked the security of the rope and returned the tools back to the workshop. He then went back inside and closed the doors and shutters went through his shut down procedure. He looked out of the back door and the snow had now carpeted the whole yard and was still falling heavily. When he awoke the next morning the snow had totally engulfed the landscape and the grey laden clouds were still depositing their contents onto the Cornish Tor in blizzard like proportions. Felix opened the shutters and went to one of the upper bedroom windows and checked the surroundings using high powered binoculars. The lane had disappeared overnight and the white blanket had taken the sharp edges off of all of his geographical reference points. Felix had to juggle his childlike excitement for snowfall and his adult dread that not only would this make him a prisoner in the farmhouse but also everywhere he went he would leave tell-tale tracks. Not what you want when you are trying to be invisible. He went into the yard and cleared away a path from the Land Rover's outhouse to the main gate. It was being covered again almost immediately by the heavy snow, as long as he could keep the snow to level the Land Rover could manage he at least had a chance. He then fitted the extra grip tyre covers on the County carried out the same procedure up the lane to the top of the tor.

With this done there was nothing to do but wait it was the thing he hated most he even tried to look at the rope ladder to see if he could complete its attachment to the cliff face but it was impossible to work on level surfaces let alone on a rope ladder a hundred and fifty feet above the raging sea.

CHAPTER 18

The Prime Ministers country home at Chequers is steeped in history from the past and is located in a place called Ellesborough just south of Aylesbury in Buckinghamshire. It was given to the nation in 1917 by Lloyd -George and houses the largest memorabilia to *Oliver Cromwell* in the famous long room. It also housed the diary of Lord Nelson and many other national treasures. Due to the security implications these are not open to the public. In 1942 Churchill was moved from Chequers as it was not secure enough so it was redesigned to make it more defendable. One of these changes was to camouflage the main entrance driveway from the air. Well over two hundred staff members are employed at the site. It is a building with a stunning façade as you approach from the main driveway. Sir Henry had been directed to the side entrance.

Sir Henry had cleared the external security network and was now at the intermediary stage as his Government Jaguar was being X- Ray scanned. "Thank You Sir" the plain clothes officer said as he was waived through to the final stage, at the side entrance to the property.

Yet again Sir Henry was waved through and shown into a side room via the study." Hello Henry" said the Prime Minister of the British government, Richard Chambers, as he greeted his guest, "Come in and close the door". Sir Henry closed the door and said "Can we talk Richard?" Richard nodded as he pressed the "Do Not Disturb" sign on the outer door.

"What's up Henry you said it was urgent?" Enquired the PM "It is it looks as though one of our own is up to their neck in this Somalia business" replied Henry. The Prime Minister stared out the window before replying "How certain are you Henry?" Henry moved uneasily "I have no definitive proof yet but all roads lead to Whitehall." The PM put his hands on his head and asked "Any names in the frame?" Henry answered quietly "Not yet but they must have access to level six security clearance."

The PM looked suddenly very old and eventually he asked "What damage can this do Henry?" said Richard slowly, "If we can root him out ourselves we can keep a lid on it" said Henry confidently "What if it goes rogue?" persisted the PM "Then we are in trouble Richard."

The PM walked across the room and stared at a Constable landscape hanging on the study wall "What's the score with your running man?" asked the PM.

"He's holed up in the West Country" Henry replied "And his wife is she still held hostage?" The PM continued "Yes sir" Henry replied. "Are we on the case Henry?" The PM asked almost pleadingly as he took his seat at his ornate writing desk. "Yes sir we are very close to tracing the girl and Barnard has become quite a player" The PM put his hand on his chin and said "We need to force the issue Henry, let them know where Barnard is" "That should drive them into the open" he added now studying his shoes." I need this sorted and sorted quickly" he finished decisively. "Give me another week Richard and if I cannot trace the girl I will give them Barnard". Offered Henry. The PM weighed up this offer. "A week and that's it Henry" the PM had made his decision "Don't let me down Henry" he then stood up and Henry knew the meeting was over. They both stood up "I'm sorry about this couple Henry but I must look at the big picture" he shook Henry's hand and walked back into the study and closed the door. That was worse than Henry had hoped for he now had a week to trace Belle and set Felix on the trail.

The prime minister made a private call to a number" Hello darling" he said "Something has come up I will have to cancel our meeting this evening" The answering voice sounded desperately disappointed "Are we still okay for the weekend"? There was a pause "I was so looking forward to it." "So was I" answered the PM." Anything I need to worry about Richard"? The PM paused again a lot longer this time. "I will sort things out you don't have to worry" he said reassuringly. "That's good darling" came the reply. "I must go now I will see you at the weekend" said the PM. He replaced the receiver. I hope this doesn't go horribly wrong he thought.

Henry briefed Hutchins with the need to move fast. The latest weather reports were not good heavy snow in the West Country and spreading into the Cotswolds in the next few hours. He had to trace Belle today to have any chance of putting an operation together to arrange her escape. He spent the next hour on the phone and when he arrived at his office he already had some answers.

Every property in Moreton on the Marsh and the surrounding district had been checked for recent lets and only six fell into the category that would suit a kidnap team. Firstly as remote as possible, have enough outbuildings to house escape vehicles and one that was easily defended. His team were able to visit four of the properties on the short list and all had bona fide tenants.

The weather was just starting to break when the Cotswold Electric Contracting Land rover called at the charmingly named Devilsgate Farm. The tenant answered the door and was only too keen to let the team check the main fuses and the pylons at the rear of the property. To the casual eye there was nothing amiss here but to the experienced eye there were too many locks and chains on the outhouses, the high powered radio aerial on the barn and most oddly no sign of animals.

My mate used to keep Gloucester old spot up here" said the pretend electrician "Do you keep any?" "I see you have specially built houses for them" he continued. The tenant looked generally in the direction of the yard "Did he" he replied non-commitally. "They do really well on the Cotswolds" continued the pretend electrician to the pretend farmer. "I notice you haven't got any stock at the moment are you waiting for the spring"? The pretend farmer was by now starting to look less than enamoured by the pretend electrician's Spanish Inquisition style of questioning." I really appreciate your interest in my farming plans for the future and when I do stock this farm I will write to you for advice "he said menacingly." Alright mate I was only trying to help" said the pretend electrician retreating to his van.

As they sat in the van his colleague said "Did you notice his hands"? The driver nodded. "More at home on a typewriter than a plough" was his comment. The electricians left and the tenant went in and closed the door before they pulled away. "He knows about as much about farming as my Aunt Fanny" he chuckled "That much" his colleague replied.

The area was targeted within the hour and Hutchins was informed, he needed to contact Felix immediately so he had a two words added to the six o clock shipping forecast. The words "I'm sorry" were inserted prior to the words Dover, White, Portland and Plymouth.

CHAPTER 19

The message was received by Felix who listened to both transmissions of the shipping forecast every day. He fitted a new SIM to another new mobile and phoned the emergency contact number.

"Hello" said Hutchins" you got the message" "Yes" replied Felix "Have you found her?" "We have" replied Hutchins "Location" asked Felix "The Cotswolds, Moreton on the Marsh" said Hutchins. "Is she alive?" asked Felix "I don't know" said Hutchins, what is the weather like where you are?" Heavy snow" replied Felix. "Be ready at first light" said Hutchins "Give me your postcode" he added" PL09 6BJ" said Felix. "We need to find a place to land so set up a landing area and mark it out with flares" he went on "We will let you know when we are near so you can light the flares". "Try to keep the snow depth to a minimum but we will have snow skis fitted". "Will do" said Felix "Till tomorrow" said Hutchins and the phone went dead.

When Felix put the phone down he could not stand still, he was like man possessed he checked his Glock 23 handgun and his Heckler and Goch automatic rifle. He knew he needed to get a good night's sleep so he would be in prime condition in the morning. He also knew there was no way he would sleep tonight so he checked his ammunition belts and laid out his clothing for the following day. He was sure if the weather stayed as it was that they would bring whites, he just had to be sure to lay out the thermal undergarments and socks. He dug out his long reach studded snow boots and snow goggles. Nothing now to do but wait. He tried to remember the main points of his crash training course he had received at Hereford. Stay low and move slow on the way in. Squeeze triggers slowly without jerking to maintain accuracy, plan your approach so as not to put your own comrades in the firing line. Automatic weapons are effective but indiscriminate. Automatic weapons show up against the snow. Snippets of his training kept coming back. "I will never remember it all" he said out loud.

As he knew there was no long sleep just fitful dozing in the chair by the fire. The snow continued into the night and the temperature started to drop quickly and when he walked out into the yard the snow crunched underfoot and he was concerned that it would be too slippery for the helicopter to land. He checked his watch it was just coming up to five am and he placed the flares in a large circular pattern in the yard. He did think about trying to remove more snow from the landing area but decided he would only make the area slipperier than it already was. At five thirty am he heard the distant sound of an approaching Eurocopter Dauphin and his phone rang "Its Go" was the message. Felix lit the flares." *I am on the way Baby just hang on"*

The helicopter landed without mishap and they were back in the air and flying out to sea to avoid flying over any inhabited areas.

The cold weather and the snow had reached Moreton on the Marsh and the temperature in the barn was only just above zero. The work on the stone blocks had been a slow arduous progress but one block was now not attached to the wall and the adjoining block was very loose. Another day she thought and the space will be just big enough to crawl through. Any escape would have to be attempted at night as the wall faced onto the main yard. Since the first stone had become loose Belle was able to see the layout of the yard by removing the stone and looking out at night. She had had to stop her digging tonight due to the cold. Even the chemical toilet had frozen up. She climbed back onto her fold up bed and pulled the thin blanket around her. It was a good job there were no mirrors here she thought she must look a real sight. Her clothes stank and she hadn't washed for over a week and this was cold water in an old bowl with no soap. Her hair had grown wildly over the last months, this judgement based on the obvious winter season and her last taste of freedom was May in Alexandria, and that was at least two seasons ago.

"Don't give up on me Felix" she said as she cuddled up in the blanket.

CHAPTER 20

The Eurocopter Dauphin helicopter made the journey to the woods four miles away from the Devilsgate Farm and landed in a clearing in about seventy minutes. It was now 16th February 2010.

A Land Rover was waiting and as Felix expected they were now clad in snow gear. The team consisted of six SAS commandoes and Felix and were commanded by a full Major.

The Major had briefed them on the flight and they landed and boarded the Land Rover that drove them to a wood adjacent to the house.

They approached the farm over land two fanning out to the rear one to approach from each side and two to approach from the front. These two led off in advance giving the building a wide berth

"I expect they will have sensors set around the perimeter"

"But the heavy snow may make them ineffective"

He smiled wryly "If we are lucky."

We waited for the signal that the outreach teams were in place.

"She will likely be in an outhouse" he said quietly.

"Benson take the main door, Williams you take the side door to the yard"

"Yes sir" they nodded and then vanished into the snow.

"You young man will come with me and we will take the outhouse buildings."

Felix looked at his watch it was almost seven am and the snow was still falling thickly it was the perfect cover. Just then their luck ran out. The sensors they hoped would be made ineffective by the snow proved their worth.

68

There was a sudden burst of automatic fire from one of the rear bedroom windows that kicked up the snow about a foot in front of them.

"Lay still" the Major said quietly.

"Upstairs right Benson"

"Got him sir" came the soft reply.

The man at the window opened fire again and I thought we were goners But Benson was as good as his word and the gunmen fell back as Benson fired.

Felix looked around the building and he could see the hint of movement at least two more of the ground floor windows and he knew when they broke cover they would be easy targets.

"Move" said the Major making for the cover of the nearest outbuilding.

As they reached the edge of the building the whole place seemed to become a wall of sound, bullets ricocheted off the wall around them and a gunman appeared from the outhouse opposite but the Major was too quick for him cutting him down with two quick shots, other gunmen then appeared from the front of the house and one was making for the outhouse opposite.

Felix raised his Heckler and Koch fired a barrage of shells that stopped the man in his tracks, one of his colleagues behind him realised Felix had broken cover and he had him in his sights, but Benson picked him off with one shot leaving a dark red mark where his face had been.

There were now shots coming from the flanks as the Majors team picked off their perimeter defence team.

The Major was drawing fire towards him while his team were picking them off one by one. Two more gunmen were up on the first floor windows and the Major was hit as he tried to move forward, Felix saw red and opened his Koch up at the upstairs windows and was lucky enough to hit both snipers.

Felix dragged the Major behind the outhouse and threw him in what had once been a compost heap. The two members of the Major's frontal approach team had now started picking off the gunmen at the front of the building and the two flank men were catching the others in the crossfire.

"Benson try to keep them alive if you can" Felix shouted as he fitted another clip to his Heckler and Koch.

"If I can sir" he shouted back.

As the battle became less frantic Felix ran for the outhouse with the bar and padlocks and shouted "Stand back from the door" and opened fire with his Koch at the padlocks.

He pushed the door open and there was a person he did not recognize at first until she spoke.

"Felix you came" and he ran towards her and hugged her and while holding her in his arms he said" Come on my love we need to get out of here"

He reached the door first and checked the battle outside

"Benson" is it clear?"

"All clear sir" replied Benson.

"How many Casualties Benson?" Felix asked.

"Corporal Wilkins is dead sir"

"The Major is badly wounded but alive sir" he said

"I have called for the helicopter" added Benson.

Suddenly Felix had another one of his sixth sense moments.

"Get the men undercover in the trees Benson"

"What for sir I need to get the Major to hospital ASAP?"

"Just do it Benson" snarled Felix. So grudgingly they all moved off into the surrounding woods and took cover.

Within minutes the helicopter arrived, and it was not the Eurocopter they had arrived in. It was a Westland Apache without markings, and it hovered over the yard.

One of the gunmen who had been deliberately left alive by Benson waved his arms for assistance, the six men in the helicopter opened fire killing anything that moved or even anything that didn't.

"Where the bloody hell are they?" called a voice from the cabin. "They are here somewhere find them and kill them all" said a voice as the helicopter touched down.

Six camouflaged SAS troopers piled out of the chopper and started to fan the area. "No survivors" was the shouted order from the Captain as he leapt out to join his team.

Benson looked at Felix "We know what to do sir" as the crew left the helicopter they were surrounded by Benson and his team. One by one they were picked off.

"Try to keep the Captain alive" called Felix.

"If we can sir" replied Benson.

The Captain tried to make a run for it back to the chopper, where the pilot still remained, as the chopper started to lift off Corporal Hewitt shot the pilot through the head. The chopper bounced back to earth and rocked violently sideways just as the Captain was leaping for safety. The rotor blades caught him in full flight. Even the hard bitten troopers looked away as he was chopped to pieces by the whirling Sword of Damocles.

The silence was broken only by the slowly reducing rotors, and soon even these stopped as if in respect for the carnage spread around them.

Sergeant Benson checked the chopper "This is another SAS unit not one of ours" he said.

"We have an enemy that knows exactly what we are doing Sergeant" said Felix.

Sergeant Benson checked the bodies to see if any had survived but a mixture of SAS training and modern automatic weapons had ensured there were no survivors. Corporal Wilkins body was placed into the helicopter.

Corporal Hewitt then flew the helicopter to the location that Hutchins had instructed and the Major was rushed into surgery. It was touch and go for a while but he was a tough old bird and he pulled through.

Felix was able to visit him for a few moments "Thanks Major" he suddenly realised he didn't even know his name.

"According to Benson I should be thanking you" He said weakly.

"You not only saved my life but the rest of the team as well" He was now struggling to breathe.

Felix took his hand "It was an honour to serve with you and your men Major."

He smiled again. "Call me Michael" he said as drifted off to sleep.

Felix spoke to the senior doctor, Colonel Hammersmith, and he assured him he would make a full recovery after a lengthy spell of sick leave. He thanked him and walked out to have a chat with Sergeant Benson.

"It doesn't seem right fighting against our own" Benson said shaking his head.

Felix nodded. "I agree Sergeant, but these are not our own, they are acting under the control of an evil force."

"I have seen that in action" agreed Benson.

Sergeant Benson shook Felix by the hand and said "Thank you sir" "No more needs to be said" replied Felix.

CHAPTER 21

B elle was able to "bring herself back into the human race" as she called it and had her hair cut and highlighted, her nails manicured and soaked in baths for days. They spent two weeks at the villa.

And the weeks passed with Belle and Felix spending hours catching up on their enforced absence in a villa provided for them. They spent hours wrapped up in each other's arms and were loath to let each other out of sight

"It was you that gave me the reason to go on when things seemed hopeless" she told him, "And all I thought of was seeing you again so we could cuddle each other as we have done every day since we have been together" he said, with his eyes suddenly filling with tears. She looked adoringly at the man she had loved since she was twelve years old and said "I could not believe that our life together was over "Belle said with tears now starting to stream down her face. Felix pulled her toward him and held her in his arms and kissed her passionately "We were meant to be together and it will take more than a few maniacs to keep us apart". She nestled into his arms and said seriously "We will make it through this won't we darling"? "Of course we will" he said with a confidence he did not completely believe.

They lay together enjoying the emotional and physical re-joining of the Barnards. Their lovemaking had taken on an extra intensity since their forced separation and both were now totally uninhibited, this did cause some eyebrows to be raised when they asked for certain latex and rubber items to be brought in, as they were not allowed to leave the villa.

Belle was able to contact her family and she had to disregard her parent's insistence that she came home immediately so that they could keep her safe. Their minds were put at rest after a call from the Security Services who convinced them that she was in good hands and was in no danger.

While both Felix and Belle may not have agreed with this synopsis at least it kept the family from worrying too much.

CHAPTER 22

Felix met with Hutchins at a service station on the M1 to discuss the events at Devilsgate Farm.

Felix had two main questions and they were.

"How had the message been intercepted and rerouted to the other helicopter"? Felix asked.

"This was a closed network with only local coverage so they had to be within a five mile radius."

And finally "How did they know the location of the operation when it was a class six operation "?

"More questions than answers" said Felix.

Hutchins replied "Leave this with me.

"You and Belle lay low at the farmhouse in Cornwall".

"Do you think that the address has been compromised" asked Felix

"Only one way to find out" smiled Hutchins.

"Thanks pal" said Felix.

Hutchins was sat at his desk mulling over recent events only two people knew the location of the farmhouse and the proposed action.

One was the head of Section G who was responsible for secure clandestine communications. Gerald Vickers had been a field operative with MI6 for twenty years and was due to retire in June this year. He had known Vickers for twenty years, and since his wife died some five years ago he was a regular visitor to his own home. Nevertheless he still had to pass the test Philby and McLean were nice guys too.

Colonel Martin Whitcombe was the head of M division they were responsible for putting together attack teams. Colonel Whitcombe was an ex SAS officer who had been injured during an attack on a foreign embassy in London.

One of these was a traitor mused Hutchins. "Only one way to find out I need to use Felix and Belle as a target" he said out loud.

He composed a level six communication to each of the possible candidates, when Felix and Belle were back in Cornwall he would send a message to the first section head.

Felix and Belle returned to Cornwall about a week later and they used public transport to reach Plymouth. They then hired a car, for which they paid cash, and drove toward St Minver. The weather had abated slightly and the main roads had been cleared but the side roads were still only passable with great care.

They managed to reach about half a mile away from the farm at which point the hill and the un-cleared roads proved too much for their Ford Focus. They walked the last half mile up to their knees in snow and by the time they reached the yard they were soaked right through.

Despite the rather arduous trek they still checked the perimeter tell tales. They were able to use the Land Rover to tow the hire car up the hill and put it into another of the barns.

They lit the fire on and restarted the central heating as although the snow was only in sporadic flurries the temperature was remaining at around minus four up on the hill where the farm was.

The next few days passed without incident the weather improved enough for Felix to carry out the attaching of the slip ropes to the rope ladder almost down to the bottom of the rock face. When he reached the bottom there was a ledge which led down to the rock strewn bay. The tide covered this ledge at a very full tide but it was clear of water at most times.

They drove into Launceston and purchased a large inflatable and a twin blade Kawasaki outboard motor. They took the Land Rover down the shore and walked the inflatable down to a cove about a mile away.

After much work, using the small generator to inflate the craft, and priming the outboard Felix took the inflatable out to sea. He gave himself as much clearance as he could from the shore line as the currents were difficult to navigate.

He brought the craft into the rocky beach at the bottom of the ladder. It took some effort to keep the lightweight craft being pulled on to the rocks. He had to use the full power of the outboard to overcome the swirling waves and the craft leapt up onto the beach. For a moment he thought he had pushed too hard and the bow would hit the base of the cliff too hard but it merely slid sideways and cleared the water totally.

Once he had the craft beached he slipped the bow rope round the first loop of the rope ladder. Soon he had secured the craft onto the ladder and he rotated the bow rope and tied the aft rope he then basically rolled the craft above high tide level. They attached another heavy duty rope to the outboard and covered it in its waterproof bag and hung it next to the inflatable.

"This looks like a suicidal escape plan" he thought "But it's all we have". Belle returned after leaving the Land Rover at the top of the footpath from the cove.

After a week of allowing information to seep to Vickers there seemed to be no action thought Hutchins. Now the time was right to play his second card, so he let the information of Felix's whereabouts finds its way to Whitcombe's team. He wanted to let Felix know but he knew he had to ensure there was no other possible way that the information could have been leaked. Another two days went by still no activity and Felix was beginning to think that the threat was all in Hutchins head.

But as the light started to fail at around three thirty in the afternoon an external perimeter sensor was activated. It was not unusual to have a random activation by badgers, birds or rabbits but within the next two minutes another detector about three hundred metres away was activated.

Coincidences are things which Felix did not believe in, so he activated his defence mechanisms. He checked the perimeter area where the alarms had been triggered using his binoculars. He could just make out two or three shadows in the gloom.

They had made a fatal error in using whites as they now stood out against the darkening sky.

Felix activated his land mines in the area of the incursion. He activated the automatic firing weapons located in the roof space which were timed to fire bursts at irregular intervals from three sides of the roof.

"Let's go" shouted Felix as he and Belle now dressed in all black scurried out into the deepening gloom

He had set the explosives to detonate in five minutes so time was of the essence. They ran keeping low to the edge of the cliff and Felix let Belle start the downward climb. The weapons were firing automatically and there was returning fire coming from areas around the farmhouse.

Belle was nearly at the bottom and had started to untie the inflatable. Felix stayed at the top of the ladder in case they had company but they seemed to be held up by the roof guns.

He dropped down the rope and reached Belle who was now dropping the inflatable on to the partly covered beach. She left one rope securing the craft while Felix untied the Outboard and manhandled it onto the rear of the inflatable. No sooner was it located in the slots and locked than the outboard fired up and they leapt aboard and Belle let go of the securing rope.

They shot forward into the foaming surf and the craft bucked upwards before plunging downward and after scooping up a bow wave full of water surged forward. The first few minutes were akin to riding a rodeo horse but once they had cleared the inshore surf the progress was swift. They then turned to port and sped parallel to the beach until they reached the cove a mile along the shore. The noise of the outboard was mostly screened by the cliff face and the sound of the gunfire.

Just as they beached the inflatable at the cove there was an enormous explosion from the farmhouse. This was followed by another explosion some two minutes later; this he assumed must be the propane tanks at the side of the house. They disembarked and ran up the track to the Land Rover.

They turned right onto the lane driving away from the house and followed this lane towards Wadebridge and then onto Bodmin and Lisekard.

They had a stop off at Plymouth and the final part of their journey took them to Exeter Airport.

They stayed overnight at the Gypsy Hill Hotel about two miles from the airport.

They boarded a flight at eleven am for Dyce Airport in Aberdeen Scotland.

The flight took about an hour and forty minutes and the small Lear Jet struggled with turbulence over the large cities. But they landed safely and were through the customs channels by just after 1pm.

They caught an onward flight by Flybe to Stornoway Airport on the Isle of Lewis in the Outer Hebrides in the Western Isles of Scotland.

They reached their rented detached house by three pm 19th April 2010.

CHAPTER 23

Hutchins had now managed to isolate the mole in the Intelligence team, Colonel Martin Whitcombe MBE, a war hero and a close colleague of many influential government figures. Although he was as certain as he could be he knew he had to convince his superiors there was enough evidence to validate this.

The team used in the attack on Felix at Devilsgate Farm were all killed by the SAS team. The bodies were scrutinised and one was recognized as an Ex SAS Sergeant. There were no survivors or bodies left after the attack at St Minver, these had been removed by the attack force at the time, so the links were quite tenuous still. He knew he had to report to Sir Henry and ask his advice.

They met on the Thames embankment the following day and the conversation was brief. Hutchins explained the events that had occurred and his interpretation of them.

"We must be sure Richard" he said slowly.

"He is a bloody hero for god's sake"

"What evidence we have all points to him" said Hutchins.

"Okay Hutch put a Class 1 tail on him and tap all communications" he then added "Better use a team from outside MI6."

"Already arranged sir" said Hutchins.

"Are you sure there are no more involved?"

"I don't know sir" replied Hutchins truthfully.

"What's your plan?"

"I may need to use my running man again" said Hutchins.

"Do what you have to do Hutch" Sir Henry replied staring out across the river.

"This is a bad business, so better keep this strictly on a need to know basis." "Will do sir" replied Hutchins.

CHAPTER 24

Hutchins checked back over the records of incidents since the sighting of the yacht in Somalia. On each occasion Whitcombe had been in the intelligence loop. He knew that Felix and Belle were in Alexandria and was made aware of the hideaway in Lincolnshire in December. He was in the operation room at the time the GPS tracker found the Renault. Finally and most damningly no action was taken in St Minver until his team were involved.

"Is Whitcombe the top man "he mused" or is there another link in the chain?" One thing he did know Whitcombe was not the man on the yacht as he was in Northern Ireland at the time. "So who was the man on the yacht"? He asked again.

Sir Henry met with the Prime Minister at a small back room at the Whites Club in St James's and a security man stood guard at the door.

"Tell me some good news Henry" he said.

"We have a suspect Prime Minister.

"Call me Richard in here Henry"

"Sorry Richard" said Henry.

"Well who is it?" Asked the PM

"Martin Whitcombe" replied Henry.

"How certain are we?" The PM asked.

"Well Hutchins thinks it's certain" Henry replied.

"What's your view Henry?" said the PM slowly.

"I am certain enough to put a tail on him and tap his communications". Henry said.

"Have you checked his financial status?" the PM went on.

"It's already done Richard."

"Is he alone in this Henry?" the PM questioned.

"I bloody well hope so sir" whispered Henry.

"Was he the man on the yacht that Barnard saw?" queried the PM.

"No sir he was in Ireland" answered Henry.

The prime minister looked out of the window before finally saying.

"Who does Whitcombe have affinities with in political circles?"

"They are mostly ex-military types, those with right wing sympathies," said Henry.

"Anyone in particular"? The PM went on.

"About three from the top of my head "Henry said slowly.

"And they are"? The PM asked.

"Lord Wetherall, Sir Geoffrey Howden and Viscount Winstanton sir" said Henry.

"Check them out quietly Henry" he sighed.

"And I mean quietly" he stressed." Consider it done sir" Henry nodded.

"I need this tidied up Henry and I want it done now".

The Prime Minister walked towards the door and looked back.

"Make it happen" he then walked into the main area of the lounge.

The PM was on the phone almost immediately.

"Hello darling we need to meet up urgently something has come up"

"What has happened Richard"? She asked hurriedly.

"Not on the phone, I will meet you in the summer house tonight at seven" he replied

"I will be there" she replied putting down the phone.

She thought of how she and Richard had been lovers since his early days in politics and now due to the stupidity of another man it was all going wrong. His rise to fame had been supported financially by her family she hoped she would not have to remind him where his loyalties laid.

On his way back to his office Sir Henry contacted Hutchins and issued his directives regarding the extra surveillance duties and the kid glove techniques required. Hutchins hand-picked his team, they consisted of officers who had no connection with the MI6 operations. Now all he had to do was set up a trap that would drive Whitcombe to show his hand. He did not know that Felix had the one piece of information that would make this happen. The final showdown that Felix had spoken of was slowly gathering momentum and the end game was almost nigh.

Hutchins answered his phone when Felix rang and explained what had happened without naming either Sir Henry or the Prime Minister. "We need to find a way to push the top players into the open.

"There is one thing I haven't mentioned till now regarding the man in the white suit" said Felix

"Go on" said Hutchins eagerly

"Well, I did get a quick look at his face" he said hesitantly

"And you never thought to tell me" shouted Hutchins

"It was only a glance and anyway it couldn't be who I thought it was" he mumbled.

"What do you mean it couldn't be" "Well" said Felix "the person I thought it was is dead"

"And who pray did you think it was" said Hutchins exasperatedly.

"Well I thought he looked like Lord Anderson the ex-round the world sailor and former British Prime Minister" he said sheepishly

"But it couldn't have been he was lost at sea while sailing in the Americas Cup" he continued "I remember the news coverage at the time while I was still at sailing school."

Hutchins stared at his phone with his mouth open.

"But his body was never found and he was a former war hero" his mind was racing now.

"Ex SAS I think". He suddenly said

"Let me do some checking and I will get back to you".

The phone went dead. Belle looked at Felix. "I remember him too he was the all action hero who then made it big in politics".

She then added "But where did it all go wrong he had everything going for him" she said.

"We don't know that it was him" said Felix "It may just have looked like him "he continued. Let's see what Hutchins comes up with" "Okay" said Belle.

"Let's go for a walk along the coastal path" she said excitedly.

The snow was prevailing but not with any malice so the ground underfoot was firm and the whiteness always makes the light last longer.

They were out for an hour before the darkness started to fall and they returned to their comfortable three bed detached stone cottage.

Felix raked over the peat and coal fire while Belle started to attack the fresh food they had purchased on their arrival on the island.

The range was soon firing up and the heat started to fill the cottage. Although they had no defence plan or equipment on the island they hoped the distance and the remoteness of Lewis would give them a buffer against immediate pursuit.

CHAPTER 25

They had just completed a lamb casserole and fresh vegetables and roast potatoes when Felix's phone rang.

Hutchins could hardly control his excitement as he spoke.

"I was right Lord Anderson or Colonel Anthony Anderson as he was prior to his promotion to the House of Lords." He was still obviously excited as he carried on.

"I was also right about his background he was the senior SAS operations officer for six years" and now came his piece de resistance.

"His adjutant for the last four years was the then Major Whitcombe and he was part of the Americas cup team aboard when Anderson disappeared".

"But why would he disappear where was the advantage"? Felix said.

"Give me time and I may be able to answer that" said Hutchins.

How safe are we here?" asked Felix.

"Well so far your location is known only to me, and our continual usage and then destruction of mobiles and SIM cards will stop any tracking systems".

"I will let you get some rest and I will contact you tomorrow with any news" the phone then went dead.

"Not much on small talk is he "said Belle.

"He's got a lot on his mind my lovely" Felix replied.

"Let's enjoy a nice warming drink of a fluid distilled on the Isle of Spey" he chuckled.

With that they settled down for a restful evening, not something they were used to.

Hutchins spent the night down in the archives of his department in the city. He did not use his computer because he knew that files could be tagged so that if anyone asked for their download then a trace was activated. Although the method he chose was painstakingly slow and laborious it was he thought the safest option. "If we are right" he thought this would be bigger than the hunt for Lord Lucan and more embarrassing than Burgess and Mclean.

It was relatively easy to find information on Colonel Whitcombe as he was still theoretically a serving soldier, be that it did not involve wearing a uniform. His pay as a full Colonel and his bursary and emoluments added up to a very tidy sum per anum, well in excess of a hundred thousand pounds.

His home was a reasonably large country house not excessive and with very little land.

He had paid for this some years ago and appeared to be under no financial pressure. His bank accounts were comfortable but again not unreasonably so and he appeared to have no vices I.E. gambling or women, not even men.

"So why has he sold his country out" mused Hutchins. He did have to gamble on one trip into the phone line, but he used another new mobile and SIM. He phoned a colleague at Interpol regarding offshore bank accounts either in the Bahamas or in Switzerland. He asked them to search for both Whitcombe and Anderson and they said they would let him know if they found anything.

He moved his attention to Lord Anderson. He was the son of a Hampshire forester who had excelled at college and University. He followed his swift promotion on merit up through officer ranks in the Paratroops Regiment. He had reached the rank of a full Major before his thirtieth birthday. This marked him out for a commission in the crème de crème of the British Army. As a full Colonel he commanded the SAS hit teams who were deployed as a last resort because all normal operations had failed. Not only did he have a ninety six percent success rate but he only lost fifteen men in his six years in command.

To further advance his almost superhuman status he was also an outstanding sailor and had represented England at the 1972 and the 1976

Olympics sailing in the Laser class. He won a silver and a bronze medal respectively.

He was already a folk hero when he was coerced into becoming the Conservative Member of Parliament for Esher in 1990 at a local by election. He won with a majority of over twenty thousand votes.

Following John Majors departure in June 1995, Anthony Anderson became the surprise choice of the Tory party to replace him. He was as popular as a politician can be and his calm no nonsense approach won him admirers from all parties.

His weak point if you can call it that, was that he was a fierce nationalist, as many ex-soldiers are, and he had a very hard line when dealing with "the begging bowl of Africa and Europe" Believing we should spend our cash on "our own people." His right wing nationalist line saw some people in his own party start to distance themselves from his remarks.

After two years in office he was replaced as Prime Minister and in the New Year's honours list he was made Lord Anderson. Some cynically suggested this was part of the deal, brokered with the Chief Whip, in agreement for stepping down. So an opportunity to spend five weeks away sailing in the Americas Cup being hosted in Auckland in New Zealand, seemed the perfect respite. It was while sailing on the New Zealand entry the *Sir Peter Blake* in 1998 that he was lost overboard on a squally afternoon apparently being hit in the head as the boom swung sharply. An immediate search was made by the crew and they radioed for assistance and a recovery team were on hand in around twenty minutes but they never found his body.

The on board search party included Colonel Whitcombe who was the Prime Ministers SAS officer. He was in fact the first man over the side following the incident.

There was a state burial at Westminster Abbey and the Military were out in force saying goodbye to their hero. The politicians immediately forgot their distaste for his right wing views and spoke of him in reverential tones as one would of a member of the royal family. The public had loved him, the upper echelons because of his military service and lower because of his nationalistic views, "To keep Britain British" as he was often quoted.

Hutchins sat back in amazement. This man was revered by all that knew him and loved by the man in the street, surely Felix must be wrong. He re-checked the report of the incident with the following queries as a guide. Was he wearing a life Jacket? Why was he not wearing a safety harness? How come an experienced sailor was taken unexpectedly by a swinging boom? Finally he was an expert swimmer and diver so why didn't he not just swim to the surface?

The accident report answered some of these questions but by no means all. He was not wearing a life jacket as he was a strong swimmer and he felt it was unnecessary. The same reason was given for not wearing a safety line. The weather that day was unpredictable and the area off Auckland is renowned for sudden strong gusts of wind. So it was feasible that he was taken by surprise by the boom. It was suggested that the boom had knocked him unconscious and that he gone straight to the bottom. The water is about two hundred feet deep at the spot the accident occurred.

He found Whitcombe's statement and read it avidly. He had seen Anderson fall into the water and had shouted "man overboard" to raise the alarm. Before they had time to put about Whitcombe had dived in to find him. He came to the surface after a few minutes but was unable to find any trace of him.

Other crew members then extended the search but again without any success. They had already raised the alarm and the rescue boat arrived, with three fully kitted scuba divers, who then carried out a systematic search of the sea bed, but again without finding his body. Hutchins stared at his desk, as if expecting help from the mahogany, and so it did.

"Of course!" he shouted as he looked up to ensure he was alone, after all it was ten past three in the morning, "it's the Bettesworth Switch." So named after the successful rescue of Senator Bettesworth from the Ugandan guerrillas on Lake Victoria some ten years ago by the SAS. They fitted a polythene sheet to the hull of a yacht, it was the same colour as the hull but was not transparent, and it could be secured from either inside the sheet or externally. Senator Bettesworth was a prisoner aboard a Ugandan Princes yacht. The SAS divers set up the hull sheet and then boarded the yacht overnight put the Senator in the sheet with a separate air supply and sealed the sheet closed. They had designed the sheet to fit into the recess amidships where the effect of the current were minimised.

The Ugandans finding their hostage gone took off in all directions looking for him. He was later retrieved by miniature submarine taken to the Kenyan border and back home.

There would have been lots of time to work on the hull of the Sir *Peter Blake* as she was kept out of the water to keep her free from any fouling that might have reduced her speed through the water. Hutchins was now flying "So" he said they set up the escape sheet Anderson falls in the water and makes for the sheet, Whitcombe dives in after him, swims to the sheet, secures it from the outside and goes off pretending to search the seabed.

When he is pronounced drowned at sea the yacht is returned to its base at Auckland harbour. He is then set free, or he can release himself, and removes the sheet, and very soon there would not be any evidence of it being there, as any residue would be removed when the hull is cleaned daily.

Hutchins stood up and walked round the desk "well now I know how" he said" All I need to know is why?." Finally he checked his family, married for twenty two years to the now Lady Anderson, but formerly Victoria Anderson the daughter of Viscount Winstanton. She came from a traditional upper class background, a good rider and a socialite of the highest order. Their home Rowland's Hall in North Hampshire was a large rambling house with stables and a hundred and fifty acres of land. His wife's bank account was very healthy, and without counting her assets she had in excess of one point four million pounds in her account. He sent a heavily encrypted message to Sir Henry via Norwegian Intelligence and when he had sent it off he thought "I may even go home now".

He never saw or heard his killer; it was over in five seconds, a six inch needle pushed up into his brain via the soft tissue at the nape of the neck.

CHAPTER 26

Felix and Belle waited till lunchtime the following day for word from Hutchins. At around 3pm he phoned on another phone but there was no reply.

"This phone will always be answered" Hutchins had told him.

"Something's wrong my lovely" he said staring at his phone.

"Whatever time day or night he has answered" he went on.

"Maybe he is in a meeting" said Belle trying to help.

"He should have phoned this morning" Felix persisted, "He was so excited last night about Anderson."

"He'll be in touch darling" said Belle cuddling his arm.

"I fear the worst but let's wait till tonight" he agreed.

As they had time on their hands he went to the large multipurpose store at Stornoway bought a few electronic gadgets and Belle bought various food items and two Aaron jumpers made with genuine Aaron wool, they weighed about a stone each.

After another of Belle's gastronomic delights, they sat by the fire and Felix said seriously.

"I think the time has come for us to split up my lovely."

"No" she cried.

"Let me finish please" he said "They now know I am a threat to their organisation" He went on "They will not stop until they kill me" he paused and looked at Belle "I don't want anything to happen to you my lovely."

Belle pulled herself up to her full five feet six inches.

"When we married we swore we would look out for each other" she croaked "and I have no intention of going back on my promise" she said defiantly.

Felix looked at her and suddenly tears welled up in his eyes.

"My darling I know you would never do that" he was the one croaking now.

"But when we agreed to love one another till death do us part, I was expecting to be a little older than twenty seven" he said.

"Twenty six and a half in my case" She laughed.

They both hugged and kissed each other.

"If we go we go together" she said suddenly it all seemed to put in perspective for Felix by Belles straight forward assessment.

"Well Mrs Barnard. Its shit or bust then."

"I would rather have the bust" she giggled.

"So would I" Felix almost blushed.

Felix took a gamble and phoned a friend at his local yacht club at Eastney in Portsmouth. He was lucky to find him in the clubhouse, *"first bit of good luck today"* he thought, but then he looked at Belle, no the second obviously.

"Ben, its Felix how are you my old mate?"

"Felix I thought you were dead where in the world are you now?" he asked

"Outer Hebrides" Felix replied "I need you to phone a number for me" he went on "Why can't you phone it yourself mate?" "It's a long story" he replied "It always is with you Felix" he laughed "Give me the number and what is the message?" Felix gave him the number and the message "Uncle has passed away can you put memorandum in paper for me" he repeated the message and the number. "I really owe you one mate" said Felix "That is a least six you owe me" he laughed. "Speak to you soon Ben" said Felix "Cheers mate" and the phone went dead.

If Felix had known he was signing Ben's death warrant he would never have called him. Ben did as he was asked by Felix and then returned to the bar of the Yacht club. "Guess who I just spoke to on the phone David?" He said to the Club Secretary who was filling in behind the bar. "No idea" said David without any enthusiasm. "Felix Barnard" said Ben proudly. "Well there's a name from the past" said David now looking interested. "What's he doing now?" He asked "No idea" Ben replied "All I know is he is in the Outer Hebrides" he said raising his hands in a no idea way.

"The bloody Outer Hebrides" I thought they were going to Australia" he said astonished "Maybe they took a wrong turn" He continued now starting to laugh uncontrollably. Ben joined in "You're on the wrong tack there" They both enjoyed the joke and then David said "What did he phone you for?" "Well its funny" said Ben "He wanted me to send a message to this phone number."

"Why couldn't he phone himself?" David asked. "Search me" said Ben knocking back his pint of Ringwood Forty Niner.

David closed up the club at just after eleven that night and he recalled the last time Felix and Belle had spent an evening there and now they were sailing the world, well at least to the Outer Hebrides. He on the other hand was still running the same old yacht club. Some people have all the luck he thought.

CHAPTER 27

S ir Henry Waddington-Walker received a text message on his personal
phone regarding his deceased uncle. He knew immediately that Hutch
was out of the game.

This meant things were hotting up. He went through the message
he had received from Hutch via the Norwegians. He could not believe it
but he had to admire Hutchins logic regarding the possible "Bettesworth
Switch" and the more he thought about it, the more he started to believe
that Anderson may still be alive.

He spoke to the control Office at MI6 and asked to talk to Commander
Hutchins. "Sorry sir" he said "he is not in today and his phone has gone
dead."

"Let me know when he turns up" he said "Yes sir." as Henry put the
phone down.

He phoned another scrambled number.

"Hello" said a non-committal voice.

"This is Thor is Perseus in?" Said Henry.

"Where should he be sir?" was the non-committal voices enquiry.

"In the gods of course." was Henry's required reply.

"Putting you through now sir." the phone went dead.

After a short delay another voice came onto the line.

"Perseus speaking" came the reply.

"This is Thor. I have lost a very close uncle" Henry said.

"Did he die outside?" Perseus asked.

"No he died in-house" Henry replied.

"Do you have special instructions for the funeral?" Perseus said gravely.

"Yes, I have a young relative who is scared of catching the same illness. So I need some support for him" continued Henry.

"No problem Sir. "Perseus replied.

"Do you need any cleaning in the house?" Perseus asked.

"I need a complete fumigation." said Thor" And I want it fast."

"Will your insurance need up rating as from today Sir?" Enquired Perseus.

"Yes both Thor and Midas" said Thor.

"Consider it done sir."

Within twenty minutes all of Sir Henry's Special Branch Officers were replaced and doubled in number, as were those of the Prime Minister.

An encrypted message was sent to Perseus and all those on the suspect list acquired round the clock surveillance.

Also a team was flown to Lewis in the Outer Hebrides.

Sir Henry now felt that Viscount Winstanton had now moved into the favourites enclosure so he asked Perseus to dig into his past in more detail. He hoped his team could prevent another attempt on "Running Man."

At three in the morning they found the body of Commander James Hutchins MBE in the River Thames. The pathology team found the tiny puncture mark in the nape of the neck.

The Commissioner of the Metropolitan Police visited Leona Hutchins to break the news of her husband's death in the line of duty.

She stayed calm and said "I always dreaded this day."

"I am sorry for your loss Mrs Hutchinson Jim was a real hero, and I do not use those words lightly."

She smiled a wan smile "I would like to spend some time alone please" she said.

"Of course, if we can be of any help just let me know" the Commissioner said as he closed the front door. Leona wiped her eyes and walked back into the living room.

The door of the bedroom opened and a tall grey headed man walked in.

"Are you okay Lonny?" He asked.

"It has come as a bit of a shock" she said.

"Of course how insensitive of me" he said quietly.

She turned to Gerry Vickers, another MI6 section head and said

"At last Gerry my darling we can be together" she said rushing into his open arms.

"I wish it hadn't happened like this my darling" said Vickers.

"It may be better this way" she replied.

"He won't be hurt now will he?" She said still sobbing.

Vickers looked really sad and replied "I suppose you're right Lonny."

CHAPTER 28

"Well bloody well find out then" roared Colonel Martin Whitcombe as he paced the floor of his office in Whitehall. "They are not showing up on any surveillance system sir I think they are on to us" he quaked.

"Have you checked Hutchins team's phones?" he shouted even more irritatingly.

"Yes sir. Commander Hutchins team has been shut down sir" Whitcombe stared at the floor for a moment before he asked "Any calls in from non-security numbers?"

"Only one sir from a sailing club at Eastney in Portsmouth" he hurriedly replied.

"What was the message?" "Cannot trace sir it was sent to a direct encryption line."

"Do we have a name?" "Only Ben sir." he replied.

"Right Williams get a team down there and find Ben" he snapped "I want to know what was in that message."

"Yes sir." said Williams.

That evening three shadows visited Eastney Sailing Club found Ben and had the information Whitcombe wanted after an hour.

"They are in the Outer Hebrides Sir near Lewis" said Williams.

"Get back here I want a team off to the islands tonight, I will be coming too to see the job is not bungled again".

Ben was found the following morning when the incoming tide at Langstone Harbour washed his body onto the beach outside the garden of the Thatched House Pub. David, the Club secretary found him as he came in to open up the club. As he dragged him from the water he saw the blood stained torso and thought "This is not natural causes." He phoned the Police immediately.

Felix received a text message which appeared as gobbledegook on his screen. He removed the SIM card and placed his special card that Hutchins gave him.

The message now read "Hutchins is dead, a team is on the way to assist you, lay low." the message ended.

Felix showed Belle the message. "Oh no" said Belle" he can't be."

"I knew it" said Felix "I bloody well knew it." he went on

"Well at least we have still got someone looking out for us" said Belle. "Let's see if they really are" replied Felix.

They returned to the house and Felix rigged up some surprise packages for unwelcome guests. Then they both waited.

At RAF Lossiemouth a Sea king Helicopter left with eight fully armed Paratroopers and Whitcombe on board and headed for Lewis in the Outer Hebrides. They had an ETA of 5.30pm "we will be with them at 6pm" grinned Whitcombe

At about the same time at RAF Prestwick a Eurocopter left carrying eight SAS men and Perseus and headed for Lewis. "Make it snappy lads, we have two lives to save." He said as they boarded.

CHAPTER 29

Sir Henry met the Prime Minister at the Houses of Parliament in his chambers. "What happened to Hutchins?" asked the PM as he sat down at the walnut writing desk "He found out too much I fear." replied Henry" sitting down on an adjacent luxurious upholstered chair.

"What have you been able to find out about Whitcombe and Anderson?"

The PM asked lighting a small cigar.

"Whitcombe has offshore accounts worth millions, but we have so far found no accounts for Anderson" Henry replied trying to avoid the cigar smoke.

"Do you think he is still alive Henry?" The PM asked, while examining his cigar.

"I cannot say for sure Richard but something was not quite right about his death." said Henry slowly.

"Yes I read about the Bettesworth Switch, but what was the point, who benefitted by his death?" The PM asked as he walked to the window.

"The home and the insurance payments went to his wife" Henry said glad that the source of the smoke had moved to the window.

"Was that excessive then?" The PM asked as he walked back to the desk.

"She received a home valued at twelve million and an insurance claim of another three million." Henry replied.

"As the daughter of Viscount Winstanton who is a close friend of Whitcombe" the PM said slapping his hand on the desk.

"They were in the perfect place to plan this deception" added Henry

The PM stood up looked at Sir Henry, "Bring in Whitcombe, Henry I don't want him killing any more witnesses" the PM ordered.

"I am concerned for both your and my own safety that is why I have doubled the security sir." smiled Henry "But I will issue the order for his arrest immediately." he continued.

"What about our running man?" The PM asked stubbing out his cigar.

"Still alive. I am hoping to bring him in as soon as I can" replied Henry as he rose to his feet.

"He deserves a rest." smiled the PM. "I must go now keep me informed Henry."

"Yes Sir." replied Henry as the PM left.

This was getting serious the PM thought he had to extricate himself from this business and do it quickly. He made another call "I need to see you today" he said "you need to disappear quickly."

"What has happened Richard?" She asked. "I will explain tonight same place, same time." He put the phone down. Typical man she thought once the pressure builds they go to pieces, no balls.

As Sir Henry walked away he prayed that his team reached Felix and Belle before Whitcombe's killers did.

They should be in Lewis by now and with them both by 6pm assuming everything went according to plan. *"Where are you Anderson and what the devil is this all about?"* he said to himself as he got into his car.

Felix received an encrypted text message saying "Our ETA at your cottage is 18.00 hours do not show yourself till we signal. You will be leaving with us!" Message ends.

Felix decoded the message and explained to Belle what was happening. Although he knew the pickup team were on the way they had come too far to be caught unprepared. He set his perimeter defences checked his Glock 23 was fully loaded and he had spare clips. He had had to leave his Uzi on the mainland and he had picked up the Glock 23 and the SA80 assault Rifle which were left in a locker at the airport. He took the SA80 and left the Glock with Belle and patrolled the area round the house.

At around six ten pm he saw a Sea King helicopter flying low approaching from the east. He waited for the signal but it did not come.

Felix studied the helicopter it carried no markings not even a Military decal. This was Military intelligence he thought but not the team he was waiting for. The helicopter swooped in low over the cottage and then cruised along the front of the building. Felix had ensured there were no lights showing, and at first glance the cottage appeared deserted. The chopper came down in the front garden area and three black suited and balaclava clad figures made for the front door. At the same time two more men ran around the building to the rear to ensure there was no escape.

Felix moved towards the chopper and could plainly see another half dozen bodies still on board. He hoped Belle had followed his instruction and had left the building on his signal and made for the woods at the rear. There was a short delay before the first soldier returned and said

"This one is empty sir." At this point a large figure filled the side entrance. "When you say empty do you mean no one is living there?"

"No sir, it is in use but there is no one here at present."

"Right Wilson you and Jeffries stay here hole up in the woodland at the rear." He roared "and wait to see who comes back."

Whitcombe turned to the helicopter pilot and said "Come on the rest of you we have three more properties to check."

With that the rest of the team boarded the chopper and the other two made for the woods at the rear. Felix had told Belle to hide there too. As they made their way across the front garden area he took a completely uncalculated risk, he lifted the SA80 and took aim at the widest part of farthest black shape just below his head.

The rifle cracked loudly in the silence of the night.

He saw the first man fall but he was already targeting the second shape.

He of course had dived to the floor at the sound of the shot but he was in open ground so he still presented a partial if not full target. Felix fired at the partial target.

Felix was sure he had hit him but he could not be sure of what damage he had inflicted. He also wondered whether the gun shots had been heard in the helicopter.

He then started to crawl his way towards his targets. He found the first black figure nearest his position and he was dead, so his second shot at the partial target had found its mark.

He was just checking the body when he felt a searing pain in his left arm and saw the other figure ducking back down into the low shrub bed.

He remembered his training and just waited and held his sight arm steady. It was about thirty seconds before he saw a movement and he fired at the middle of the movement. There was a cry and then it all went quiet.

Felix crawled forward very stealthily but found the second figure was also dead. He checked his arm, just a flesh wound no serious damage.

Just then his phone received a message "ETA two minutes" Felix hurriedly replied "Have had visitors two dead, rest moved on to check other sites. Safe to land"

The Eurocopter arrived in three minutes and the rescue team, arranged by Sir Henry, landed in the front where Felix had signalled with his torch.

Perseus was updated by Felix regarding the earlier visit, and he checked over the two bodies.

"SAS" he confirmed "Whitcombe's men for sure" he said.

Belle was now with the group at the front of the house.

"Get Belle in the chopper and wait for my call to return." Perseus ordered.

"Yes sir." replied the pilot "Come aboard." he said.

Belle looked at Felix "Can't I stay with you?" she pleaded.

"Sorry Lovely." said Felix softly" It's safer if you go now." he said putting his hand in hers.

"Let's go people." shouted Perseus" Time for that later." he said helping Belle into the cockpit. Within two minutes the chopper was up and disappearing into the night.

Before it had left the ground Perseus was deploying his team.

"Taffy you take Giggsy to the cover on the West and after they land you take the chopper pilot." He said quietly.

"Barnsey you take Bungy and cover the East and the backdoor."

He then turned to Felix "You will be with me and Dusty inside the house with the lights on" he laughed "we need to let them know we are at home" he continued.

They made for the house and Perseus, good to his word, turned on the living room and the hallway lights.

"Right" said Perseus "Dusty you take the front bedroom window on the left" Dusty disappeared pronto.

"Felix you take the front bedroom window on the right." he ordered. "I" he said "will be waiting by the fire in the living room."

Within ten minutes the sound of an approaching Sea King could be heard the fully blacked up Paras were ready and waiting. The chopper saw the lights and hovered above the garden trying to contact the two men Whitcombe had dropped off.

"They are not responding Sir." said the pilot.

"I can bloody well hear that." said Whitcombe" they are either dead or prisoners." he said without emotion.

"Right let's get this sorted, Bowles, Wilson go left, Hill, Mearns go right and we three will take the front."

As soon as the chopper touched down without any delay the two flanking teams left to take up their positions.

Whitcombe gave them three minutes and then said "Right let's put an end to these amateurs once and for all." and with that they crouched low and ran towards the house in the pitch black.

The infrared sights clearly showed the approaching figures from the front windows of the house but Perseus had ordered no shooting until he gave the word.

On the flanks the four Paras had found good cover and watched the approaching SAS team via their infra-red sights but they too had been instructed to hold fire.

The frontal attack trio had reached within twenty yards of the front door when the front door opened and the lights went out.

Perseus stood in the doorway "Whitcombe it's all over give up now or you will all die."

Whitcombe never even bothered to answer except by opening fire at the open door.

Perseus who was expecting this had stepped behind the wall adjacent to the door.

He dived to the window and opened fire with his infra-red sited Uzi.

This was the signal for Perseus's team to open fire, as they were already holed up with their shots ready they were able to get the drop on their assailants.

The two flank teams were able to pick off three of the SAS team but one had made off.

Chopper Harris made his way to a point behind the chopper and disarmed the pilot in a permanent way. He removed the body and took his place in the cockpit.

He had just taken his place when Corporal Hill, from Whitcombe's team, climbed in saying "It's a bloody inferno out there we have been set up."

"I am afraid you have my son." said Chopper as he disarmed Corporal Hill in the same way.

At the front door Whitcombe's man Sergeant Dodd's was picked off by Dusty Miller from the upstairs window and another Corporal Chambers was hit in the shoulder, but he was able to roll and fire at the upstairs window killing Sergeant Dusty Miller.

Felix fired at the flash location and killed Chambers before Miller hit the floor.

Whitcombe had managed to avoid the initial fusillade of shells and rolled up under the living room window. He did not fire his weapon as this would have shown his position as Chambers had done.

He moved silently around the side of the house and made his way to the back door.

Corporal Bungy Williams was positioned in line with the back door and seeing Whitcombe he opened fire and Whitcombe fell to the floor. As Williams approached he remembered his instruction "Keep Whitcombe alive at all costs." so instead of following all his training and ensuring the kill, he approached the body. This was the last mistake he would make as Whitcombe shot him through the head from close range.

Whitcombe knew that the shots would have been heard in the house so he crawled to the side of the house and hid in the undergrowth of the vegetable garden.

He had been out thought again by this bloody infernal interfering amateur.

The boss was already furious and could not believe how hard it had been to dispose of one loose end. How did they contact him with Hutchins dead? He felt the blood trickle down his side he knew he had been hit in the chest. He heard the back door open and footsteps step out onto the footpath, the footsteps stopped he raised his Glock and pointed it towards the rear corner of the house.

Another Glock 23 was pointing at the back of his head. This Glock belonged to Perseus, he had come from the front of the house, "Its over Martin put the gun down" said Perseus.

Whitcombe looked round "I might have known you would be involved David" he said.

"We learnt our trade together and you were sloppy today." said Perseus "Now hand me the gun Martin."

"Okay David just get me up will you?"

"Major David Fuller MC helped Colonel Martin Whitcombe MBE to his feet.

"Thanks David" he said pulling a small syringe from his pocket and driving it into his wrist.

Perseus tried to wrestle the syringe from his hand but he knew it was too late.

"Sorry David it has to be this way."

"But what happened Martin you were a brave soldier and a patriot" he said.

Whitcombe was fading fast "This is not the country I fought for David." he said weakly "This is a second rate nation losing its armed forces by the day." he gasped "Some of us believe we can save this country of ours." his head slumped forward and the slight tell-tale signs of the poison showed at the corner of his lips.

"Is he dead?" asked Felix who had been alongside Perseus.

"It was probably for the best." Perseus nodded sadly.

"But we still don't know who he is working for" said Felix.

"That's for us to find out." Replied Perseus.

During this skirmish Perseus had lost Sergeant Dusty Miller and Corporal Bungy Williams both not only comrades but also personal friends of Major David Fuller and the flight back to RAF Prestwick was a very sombre affair. The mission had been accomplished and both Belle and Felix were alive and Whitcombe was dead. Nevertheless, to Perseus it was difficult to be upbeat about the proceedings.

"I am glad you two are okay." he said to Belle and Felix "but I have fought with these two guys for many years and they are like family to me."

They were flown back to RAF Prestwick before being transferred to an RAF jet that flew them all back to RAF Northolt in London.

They were given accommodation on a secure security base while their safety risk was assessed. Felix had his arm treated and strapped, it was only superficial damage and would heal quickly.

They were put up in a luxury villa with five star services. They spent their time wrapped up in each other's arms to try to make up for all the time they had been apart. "The thing I missed most" Belle said "was our continual cuddling and just the warmth of your company."

Felix was so pleased to be back in a relatively normal existence with his wife that he never let her out of his sights. "I always believed you would come and find me if it was possible. I have always believed in you" she said now with tears running down her cheeks. Felix felt the tears welling up in his own eyes as he spoke "I would never give up on you darling" I knew you would hang in there no matter what" he croaked. They fell into each other's arms and kissed passionately "I love you" Felix whispered she smiled and replied "I could not live without you." They re-joined their spiritual and their physical bonds over the next two weeks.

The death of Colonel Martin Whitcombe OBE was reported in the Obituary columns of The Times and The Guardian. His death in a tragic gunshot tragedy was a sad way for a national hero to die and a Memorial Service was to be held at Westminster Abbey.

CHAPTER 30

After a week Felix and Belle were given the okay to leave the barracks and Major Fuller had a surprise for them. They were taken to St Katherine's Dock, Marina which nestles next to Tower Bridge and moored up at the Marina was Vida Nova.

Felix was amazed to see her considering he sold her in Cyprus over a year ago. It appears he was being shadowed for a lot longer than he realised. They spent the day restocking the food store and the liquor cabinet. Felix checked her over and found her in excellent condition. In the evening they sat down after a great meal and looked back at their adventure since being snatched by pirates. Holding a glass of Jameson in his hand he looked across at Belle, "All of this because we wanted to visit Nairobi" he said "We never did get there" she laughed. "I wonder who Whitcombe worked for?" Felix said. Belle looked at her gin and tonic "From what you said he seemed to be more of a misguided patriot rather than a crook"

"I think you are right my love." he said.

Just then a voice called "Ahoy there."

Felix walked up on deck and there stood a tall distinguished man in sailing gear.

"Hello its Felix isn't it?"

"Yes" replied Felix warily.

"My name is Henry, we have spoken over the phone." he replied.

"Sir Henry" said Felix" welcome aboard Sir."

"Just Henry will do." he replied.

"Come aboard." Felix said.

They walked into the cabin and Felix introduced Sir Henry to Belle.

"Can I offer you a drink?" asked Felix as he showed Henry to his seat on a heavily upholstered ivory leather armchair.

"A glass of malt would be fine." replied Henry as he sank back into the sumptuous chair. Felix provided the said beverage and both Belle and Felix joined him as it would have been rude not to.

"This is the Home Secretary Sir Henry"

"Just Henry" he interrupted.

"What can we do for you Henry?" Felix asked.

"I need to talk to you about your sighting of Anthony Anderson." he said.

"Tell me exactly what you saw."

"Well" said Felix "I saw a man of medium build about six feet tall wearing a white suit and a straw hat."

"Are you sure he was six foot tall?" asked Henry.

Felix thought to himself for a moment.

"Difficult to say. I only caught a brief glance of him."

"Was he alone?" asked Henry

"There were two people with him I think." said Felix slowly.

"Can you think of anything that you have missed?"

Felix stared into space trying to remember anything else about the brief glance he got.

"Did you see him leave the ship?" asked Belle trying to help Felix's memory.

"As I lay in the water he was going down the gang plank. In fact it looked as though he stumbled down it."

"Did it look to you as if he fell?" asked Henry.

"No" said Felix suddenly "It looks as though he was being pushed" he gasped "He was being manhandled ashore" he continued.

"This puts a different picture on the whole thing" said Henry. "It seems that Anderson is only a pawn in the game" he said.

All three present stayed silent as they took this new turn of events in.

Whitcombe's boss was indeed furious that several assassination attempts on two amateurs had failed, especially as they were purportedly carried out by professional killers.

They should have been killed in Alexandria and it was only her father's decision to kidnap the girl and not just kill the pair of them then that had caused further trouble. The loss of Whitcombe was unfortunate, but there were always casualties in every war and this is what this was.

What was important now was how many people Hutchins confided in before he was silenced. Sir Henry Waddington-Walker was obviously one and that bloody Major Fuller and maybe even the Prime Minister himself.

Things had gotten out of hand because of one piece of really bad luck. Still the need to dispose of any possible witnesses was the first step and the easiest target would be Barnard.

Apparently he had his yacht returned to him and it was moored at a marina in London. A phone call was made to a London Barracks and the instructions given "Fourth time lucky I hope" the boss said with feeling.

Sir Henry met with the Prime Minister in a meeting room at ten Downing Street.

"Are you telling me now that you think Anderson is being held captive?" said the PM incredulously as he sat behind his working desk.

"Certainly seems that way." said Henry sipping from the coffee he had been given.

"But why?" The PM asked.

"I don't know." said Henry "But I am checking his movements just prior to his apparent death" continued Henry.

"And what have you found?" said the PM testily.

"Well" said Henry "He spent a lot of time at his bank in central London"

"And?" the PM snorted.

"Well he was going over his accounts with his personal advisor." Said Henry hurriedly.

"But we have checked his accounts there is nothing suspicious there" snapped the PM.

"Maybe we need to look again" Henry replied.

"Well do it Henry. This is becoming wearing" said the PM scratching his head.

"Will do sir." said Henry.

"By the way what about speaking to his personal advisor?" the PM enquired.

"Cannot do that. He was found in the Thames the same as Hutchins" said Henry quietly.

"My god" gasped the PM "How deep does this go?" The PM was about to leave the room when he turned and said "By the way Henry, good work regarding Whitcombe. Most probably the best all round." With that he walked out of the room.

CHAPTER 31

---◆---

Felix was standing on the bow of Vida Nova admiring a Dutch ketch that was moored two berths down.

"Have a look at this Belle" he called. She came up from the cabin.

"What a beauty" she cried looking at the shape of the hull and the elongated sail.

"How is your arm feeling?" she asked.

"Still a little sore but no long term damage" he replied. The bullet that clipped his arm on the isle of Lewis seemed a lifetime away.

"Let's go out for a sail." said Belle "The tide is full and we can get to the outer reaches of the Thames" she said excitedly.

They sailed from the marina at ten in the morning and by one pm they had reached Canvey Island. The outgoing tide made their voyage both swift and effortless.

They moored up and strolled along the outdated seafront area and the oddly named Dutch streets. These streets were named after the Vikings who landed at Canvey Island in an age when the east coast was continually being invaded by the infamous Vikings. There was a real untouched feeling about the sea front area which had seem to have been locked into a time warp as if the twenty first century had not troubled with it at all.

They walked along the tatty buildings and the now seaweed covered shoreline and headed towards the little clutch of recreational buildings. Only a few remained open and Belle refused Felix's offer of jellied eels and they both ate pie and mash at a little corner cafe.

It was good to be out enjoying normal things after the horrendous times they had endured recently, and they were able to relax as they walked casually along the rather neglected seaside area.

As they walked from the cafe arm in arm a bullet hit Belle in the stomach, she fell to the floor as did Felix, and he felt for his Glock and tried to roll Belle out of the target line.

"Stay flat" he whispered. She was holding her side and he could see the blood seeping onto her hand. She grimaced but pulled her Glock from her bag.

He looked from behind the sturdy wood support to the lean to structure they were hiding in.

He could see no movement; he guessed the sniper must be in the reeds at the edge of the estuary. Slowly he moved away from Belle trying to draw fire away from her. Nothing stirred in the reeds as he moved further into the main footpath. His eyes were trained like a hawk on the area and his hand trembled with anticipation.

He was beginning to think he had been wrong when he saw a glint of light and he fired without hesitation.

The bullet hit something he could her the soft thud of its contact and for a moment he thought he had pulled off a spectacular shot, but the gunman was rolling into a gap in the reeds to fire again, this time Felix thought I'm in the open he won't miss.

He saw him line up his rifle and the repeated crack of a gunshot made him think it was all over, but he was still alive.

The sound he had heard was Belle taking out the gunman with her own Glock automatic.

He checked that he was not just nearly dead but really dead, and then rushed back to Belle and her wound. The bullet had passed through her lower rib cage but he could see no exit wound.

He called for an ambulance and held her in his arms and said to her "You are not bloody well going to die on me now."

The tears were running down his cheeks "We have been through too much to let it end like this." he held her tight as he dare.

Although she was conscious she was starting to drift off and he continually talked to her "Hang in there darling don't give up on me now, please."

Eventually the ambulance arrived and the Paramedics took over and she was taken into theatre thirty minutes later. After surgery the doctor said she was in no danger.

"Well" Felix smiled wryly "that's not quite the case all the time she is with me she is in danger."

Major Fuller arrived with a "Caretaking team" for them.

Belle was cleared to go home three days later and they returned to Vida Nova with their babysitters in tow.

The bullet had entered via the lower rib cage at a downward angle and had broken a rib on entry but it had missed the bladder and the intestines and had embedded itself in the left buttock.

"It will be very sore for a week or two but you will make a full recovery." was the verdict of the consultant who removed the bullet.

Felix would not let her out of his sight for the next few days and the thought of losing her had only intensified how much he loved her.

"I am as tough as an old boot" laughed Belle as she lay out on her deck lounger.

"I can see your tongue poking out" chuckled Felix as he kissed her gently.

CHAPTER 32

---◆---

Sir Henry met the PM at The Houses of Parliament in the same room they used last time.

"Hello Henry." said the PM pointing to a chair at the desk.

"Another attempt on running man?"

"Afraid so sir." Henry replied as he sat down.

"Are they both okay?" asked the PM looking out the window.

"They seem to have nine lives Richard" Henry replied following the PM's eyes to the window.

"Just as well." He replied.

"What can you tell me about Anderson?"? Asked the PM as he now stared unblinkingly at Henry.

"It appears he was looking into his wife's Victoria Anderson's accounts" Henry said equally seriously.

"Aren't they the same as his?" The PM asked suddenly interested.

"No she has several offshore accounts" Henry replied

"What sort of figures are we looking at?" asked the PM

Henry spoke slowly as if to stress the importance of the figures.

"Well in excess of eight million pounds in the accounts we can verify so far"

"Bloody hell" gasped Richard suddenly springing to his feet and Henry continued.

"And there may be more but they have covered their tracks well"

The PM put his hands on his head "We need to talk to her Henry pull her in." said the PM shortly.

"She is in Africa at the moment, as is her father Viscount Winstanton"

"Have we checked his offshore accounts?" asked the PM as he walked back to the window.

"Yes sir, well over twelve million pounds in the two accounts we have traced so far."

"So it's a family affair" mused the PM.

"Looks like it Sir." said Henry.

"Did you get any joy with his other contacts?" Asked the PM.

"They are all very wealthy men sir." Henry replied.

In the same league as Winstanton?" Probed the PM.

"Well, Geoffrey Howden is the richest of the others with a personal fortune of around 2 million"

"I want them in custody as soon as possible." The PM ordered.

"Yes sir "replied Henry. The PM left without another word.

Things were going from bad to worse thought the PM at least he told Vikki to get out of the country. Although he had been having an affair with her for many years he never realised that she and her family were tied up in so many not just illegal activities but piracy and murder. Because they were wealthy and bastions of the acceptable society they had funded his rise to success and he was grateful for that. He had on occasions let details slip of possible investment opportunities prior to them being public knowledge. He also was happy to continue his affair with Vikki Winstanton as she was a wild and erotic lover. He had spent many happy hours in the stable block as he trained his filly to take commands. It seemed that both she and her father had completely lost the plot and they had now become dangerous.

Time to bail out of this situation he thought. It was interesting how Vikki reacted when her late husband was not with sorrow or affection but with disgust and disdain. It would be better if the family were eliminated it would be for the best he decided. He must convince Henry that was the preferred course of action.

Major Fuller visited the following morning. "We are off to Africa Felix and you are coming with us." he said.

"What about me?" said Belle sadly.

"I am sorry Belle, but this is going to be very dangerous." Fuller said softly.

"We are going into the pirate's lair."

Felix took her hand "I wish more than anything that I could take you with me, but you need to rest. You have already proved your courage and you need to rest up after your wound"

"Felix is right, it's time for you to get yourself better, you have done more than anyone can ask." Said major Fuller smiling at Belle.

Although she felt somehow cheated as if she was missing out on the final countdown, she reluctantly agreed to miss out on this one.

"You come back to me or I will never speak to you again." she said holding Felix tightly. Although she was smiling he could see the tears welling up in the corner of her eyes.

They flew from RAF Brize Norton to Nairobi where they were met by two divisions of Paratroopers and two divisions of Royal Marine Commandoes. They had at their disposal several assault helicopters that were fully armed.

The RAF were to fly sorties over the harbour and photograph the area Felix had found and decide what type of armaments would be necessary. The aerial photos showed a similar set up to that that Felix had reported on his visit. It was decided to go in with helicopters alone.

Three choppers would land at the edge of the deepest part of the inlet and set up covering fire for the assault team. Another two would land on the both sides of the inlet at east and west sides. Four more would fly into the harbour and be the assault team. The team waited until sunset to make their attack. They received their shots of the harbour within the hour and the layout was as Felix's report.

There were still plenty of expensive craft moored up but no sign of the luxury yacht. The camouflage nets obstructed a clear view of the mooring area and the repair yard.

At five pm on 2 March 2010 they attacked the Devils Cove as it was known to the locals. The flanking teams opened fire on the defence teams and the leading choppers flew into the cove.

They put up quite a fight but they were hopelessly outgunned and outnumbered and within twenty minutes the Devils Cove was taken.

Felix landed with Fuller and they made for the hidden villa to see if it held any clues. The property was beautifully decorated and at the rear they found an ultra-modern office with a radar scanning system and a full shipping itinerary.

This also included colour photographs of all craft on the list. There was no link to who managed the operation.

There was some joy from the ten or so prisoners taken all of whom were ex Royal Navy or Royal Marines. They had been hired via a web site and were sent a ticket to fly to Mombasa, where they were picked up by cruiser and brought to Devils Cove. They never met their employer as they were not allowed into the villa. They did meet the site gaffer an ex-Marine Sergeant Tug Wilson a big burly Welshman. He had left a week ago to pick up some supplies from Aden.

Major Fuller radioed back his report and a team of Marines were sent out to scout the area for any pirate camps that may still have hostages. Plans were made to contact the vessel owners so their craft could be returned to them. MI6 tried to trace the website owners but the site was based in different places at different times and never returned to the same locations. But the boffins and the hackers were on the job.

Asked about the luxury yacht they said it arrived about every three months, but the occupants were taken to the villa and stayed there till they left about two days later. They did say that it did appear that one man was under restraint and that all the team looked European.

When the paratrooper teams returned they found five more hostages but even more importantly they found Domingo the chef at the villa. Although his English was poor they were able to get a good description of the four visitors that called at the villa.

The first man nearly six foot grey haired wearing steel framed glasses.

"Always a nice polite man." He said

"He was never left alone." He added.

The others consisted of a large muscular man.

"With tattoos all over his arms." remembered Domingo "He never said much just stayed with the first man."

The next one was an elderly gentleman expensive clothes obviously a rich man.

"He appeared to be in charge." Domingo added.

The fourth person was a woman blonde hair well dressed "Very attractive" Domingo said bashfully.

"But she seemed to be continually rebuking the first man."

"They made him leave when they wanted to talk. But he did hear the older man say to the first man you are lucky we left you alive. The first man did not look grateful for his pardon" smiled Domingo.

After digging through the paperwork they were able to come up with their modus operandi.

They made plans in the office for future "shipping acquisitions" as they called them and also arranged for repatriation dealings usually with third parties.

In addition to this the business owned Transasian Marine Ltd, which had a full order book carrying goods to and from India and the Far East. They had five vessels in their fleet with another under construction in Srilanka.

Then there was the Ocean Insurance Company that took high risk claims, at the appropriate High costs, for vessels travelling these dangerous waters.

Finally there was the disposal of sailing craft of all sizes to the appropriate bidders, those who asked no questions, at 75% face value.

Fuller looked at Felix "My god this is so much bigger than I thought." he said incredulously.

"There may be more harbours." said Felix "Can we ask the RAF to scan the whole coastline?"

"Better check with London." Fuller said "Don't want to cause an international incident."

Fuller reported in regarding what they had found and requested a full shore scan.

CHAPTER 33

Sir Henry sat on the park bench on a cold March afternoon looking across to the Serpentine when he was joined by the PM. They both sat looking ahead "Well Henry" he said slowly.

"Whitcombe is dead, it seems Wincanton and Victoria Anderson are in it up to their necks."

The PM sighed "What about Howden?"

"Still checking, some of the Swiss gnomes can be particularly obstructive." Henry replied

"Any idea where Wincanton and Anderson are?" Asked the PM watching a duck fly across the lake.

"Not at present but they still have a lot of clout with the Army Richard so be careful." he said gravely.

"Thanks Henry. I will be happier when they are both either in custody or dead" he said tightly. They both walked opposite ways as they left Hyde Park.

Sir Henry reached his office and checked for an update on the whereabouts of father and daughter. Wincanton and his daughter had flown from Stanstead, in his own Lear jet, the previous day at eight am. Their destination was logged as Budapest but they never arrived.

An airport and port search had been in place since three pm yesterday afternoon. *Where would they go?* thought Henry. *Where do they virtually own the place?* he mused. "Must be Kenya, Somalia, Ethiopia, the Yemen or Aden" he said triumphantly. He had the search centred on these countries.

Henry suddenly remembered the PM's words either in custody or dead. He agreed it was easier to make up an obituary than have a damning court case.

On the remote island of Socotra situated one hundred and fifty miles South West of Ethiopia Lord Wincanton and his daughter Victoria Anderson sat on the veranda of their palatial villa looking out to the Indian Ocean.

They had landed at Socotra Airport the previous evening and their air conditioned limousine was waiting to take them on their Villa at Stera on the South of the island.

The southern area of the island is well away from even the few hard-core tourists who attempt a visit to this island. Since having this villa built with the blessing of the former President of the Yemen *Ali Abdulla Saleh,* they used this place as the perfect getaway. It was within range of all their business interests and yet was so low profile it was almost invisible.

Wincanton was standing by the wall looking out sea when he turned to his daughter and said.

"I can't believe it has all gone wrong over one man." he was shaking as he spoke.

"It's all right daddy, but you should have let us kill them both when we had the chance." she said putting her arm around him. "We aren't finished yet." she said with conviction.

"Things are going from bad to worse. I did not want any more blood on my hands" he said.

"They will take all the vessels from Devils Cove" he sighed "Not to mention the money it cost to bring in all the maintenance and repair equipment" he continued.

"Stop it daddy! you are starting to sound like a spoilt child." She chided.

"We will find a way out of this. All we have to do is get rid of that idiot and his wife and then sir Henry and the Prime Minister."

"Are you totally mad Vicky can you hear yourself?" he raved "You want us to murder the Prime Minister and the Home Secretary?"

He stared at his daughter. I am beginning to think I don't know you at all" he said.

"If you haven't got the stomach for it you shouldn't be involved, those two are traitors of the realm and they will be made to pay for their treason too" she said angrily.

"I wanted to make money so we could make Britain great once again, I wanted to fund those people who still held our values." he shouted. "Not to murder members of the British government."

He looked tenderly at his daughter.

"It's over Vicky" he said "We have enough money to lay low the rest of our lives" he pleaded.

"In your case daddy that won't be long" she said removing a Browning pistol from her bag.

"What are you doing Vicky!" he cried.

"We are family the same flesh and blood."

Vicky shook her head "No daddy I am afraid your blood has turned to water, you don't have the guts for the fight."

She then shot him twice in the head.

She called for "Tug" Wilson to help her throw Lord Wincanton into the Indian Ocean. She went into her office and sent a letter and an instruction to her still loyal followers in the military. They had committed treason she thought and they must pay the price. She smiled as she replaced the receiver meeting out justice was always rewarding she thought.

She stormed back into the living room and looked across at her husband sitting on a large settee. "What are you smiling at?" she shouted

"You have finally lost it altogether" he laughed

"I am surrounded by lily-livered cowards" she ranted on "None of you have the balls to take on the real challenges" she continued.

Even Richard had asked her to lay low as soon as things started to hot up. He had not been so slow to turn up for his twice weekly sex romp in the stables had he? They were all the same, well they were all going to get the same as her father had. She was going to kill the lot of them. She suddenly laughed out loud at the prospect of all the men in her life begging for mercy before she blew their brains out.

Anderson stared at his deranged wife. "You started to lose it eleven years ago when you used my name to build a private army, without telling me." He said.

"We both had the same vision to ensure we kept Britain for the British and not the hangers on from every other country in the world." She screeched.

"But I wanted to do it with the support of the people and the government" he said. "I wanted to do it the right way" he finished.

"You always were naive Tony" she hissed. She turned to "Tug" Wilson "put him in the back room Wilson and make sure he's secure."

"Yes Ma'am" Wilson said.

Vicky made a phone call to England "Hello its Vicky. I am afraid Daddy is dead he started to panic" she said

"That was silly Vicky" was the reply" Have you disposed of the body?"

"In the Indian Ocean" was her reply.

"Just sit tight while I see who we can still trust" the voice said. "What about the business?" she asked

"We have enough money in accounts all round the world to buy any business we want "the voice said "So wait as instructed" the voice ordered.

"What about Sir Henry and the Prime Minister?" She persisted

"Leave them to me; you do as you have been told!"

With that the phone went dea

The voice put the phone down and cursed the decision to use this slightly unbalanced upper class family. They did of course have the connections in the armed Forces they needed but with that came this patriotic "I want to change the world" philosophy. This of course worked well with the military types and ensured their compliance. When of course the only real objective was to make lots and lots of money, and this had been achieved in abundance. She also knew Victoria would shag anyone she could if they could be of use to her family. She could say she had shagged two Prime Ministers she was not the only one.

Sir Henry asked for a sweep of all countries airports for the destination of the missing Lear jet. All the main airports had been checked and there was no report of any arrivals anywhere. The sweep was then switched to minor airstrips.

The report on Sir Geoffrey Howden was in. He was indeed a billionaire, but he had been a billionaire for thirty years, since he invested in a company called Microsoft. He did not seem to have any connections with the services although he was right wing in his views. He kept his tail anyway just in case.

The report from Devils Cove was pretty much as expected but the analyst's estimate of the profits from the enterprise over the last ten years was around sixty million pounds. These were figures that would warrant murder as a protective measure.

We must find Wincanton he said to himself out loud.

He sent an encrypted message to the PM. He was at a charity ball with his wife Danielle Chambers who was the founder member of *"Homes for our Heroes"* an institution that helps support members of the armed services during and after their service life is over.

Felix and David Fuller were due to fly back to London when they received an instruction from Henry to fly their teams to HMS Devonshire and to billet there until further notice.

Belle was able to visit her parents in Lymington and was able to relax and recuperate following her gunshot wound. She visited the Sailing Club and some of her old friends. And she thought of Felix every day.

The voice passed on instructions to a specialist team and they were kitted up and ready to move within the hour.

"This will tie up yet another loose end" the voice said out loud.

"What was that?" asked the voices partner.

"Oh nothing darling" the voice replied.

Sir Henry received a report regarding a Lear jet landing at Socotra Airport and this tallied with the target information.

"We are closing in." he said quietly. He made the phone call to HMS Devonshire.

The PM received the call from Henry and a smile spread across his face "Thank God it's almost over." he sighed.

"What was that Richard?" His wife asked.

"Sorry darling, just thinking out loud."

Felix and David were given their instructions and the destroyer made full speed for the island of Socotra. The choppers would meet them in Aden as the island was out of range of their present location. ETA for Aden was six hours. "We should be on the island by three pm local time" said Fuller.

The two blacked out choppers landed in the garden area at the rear of the villa at Stera at midday local time. The eight soldiers leapt out of the chopper fully armed.

Sergeant "Tug" Wilson saw the danger first and ran to pick up his Uzi. He opened fire taking out the first three attackers before he was killed outright by two rounds from an SA80 assault rifle.

They made their way into the living room where Victoria Anderson met them, Uzi in hand; she mowed down another two of the assault team.

The third one shot her between the eyes, and she fell to the floor.

The remaining attackers moved into the back room where Anthony Anderson was being kept prisoner.

Anderson stood up as the two armed raiders entered the leader moved towards Anderson and saluted.

"Colonel Anderson Sir" Anderson put out his hand and shook his hand warmly.

"Hello Jack" said Anderson "How are the boys keeping?"

"Very well sir." he smiled "it's great to see you again sir."

"Well" said Anderson "let's get out of here."

The bodies were loaded onto the chopper and taken for disposal.

When Alex and David reached the villa some three hours later there was no one there. The tell-tale blood stains showed signs of action but other than knowing that Wincanton, Victoria Anderson, Tug Wilson and Anthony Anderson had arrived by air they had no clue as to what happened there. They assumed that they had all been disposed of.

Sir Henry did not care which hit team had done the job as long as Wincanton and the two Andersons were dead.

The Voice heard the information and smiled *"Great no loose ends."*

The PM heard the news and thought politically, and even more importantly personally, a good result *"No loose ends."*

CHAPTER 34

Anthony Anderson made his way back to the country he loved more than anywhere else in the world. He was flown by helicopter back to Oman where he had long time allies in the government.

He took a standard Etihad flight from Muscat to Amsterdam arriving two days after he left Socotra. He was back in England the following day landing at RAF Odiham in Hampshire.

He was driven to "The Old Vicarage" a very large detached house in the village of Rowland's Castle in Hampshire. The house had a high brick wall surrounding it and automatic steel gates at the entrance drive.

He looked across at Staunton Park where the deer run free in over a hundred acres of woodland interspersed with grass avenues. He remembered his childhood working with the Staunton Saw Mill team making chestnut paling and binding hazel fencing.

He only wanted people in the future to have the opportunity to love this country the way he did. Thank god there were still people who cared about this battered but beautiful island. He hoped it was all over now and he could go back to enjoying his life sailing, walking living a normal life and being with his family. He had missed so many years of watching them grow from children into adults.

His father never called them children or kids when he was young, they were just young people. His father was a simple honest man who loved both people and the countryside equally, and he had been his hero for as long as he could remember. They may not have grown up in a wealthy home but it was full of love and understanding. His father never tried to talk him out of a career in the Army, even though his academic achievements meant he could have had a career in the city. He took him into the forest and they stood beside a three hundred year old oak tree.

"Use this tree as your example Anthony, you must have strong roots, you must stand tall, but you must remember to be part of the forest, and finally you must be yourself".

He knew more than any man he had ever known and he had been superb with his children when they were young. The three younger children loved to stop with granddad. Anderson's eldest son Andrew hated the country and thought his granddad was a country bumpkin and never visited. This only adding to the tension between father and eldest son.

He was mortified when his dad died and as his mum had died when he was very young and the cottage was passed on to him. He had it modernised in equipment but the look and the layout stayed exactly as it was when he grew up there. This was no shrine, this was a place to enjoy visiting as it brought back warm and wonderful memories.

He picked up the phone and phoned the voice "I am home and free." and replaced the receiver.

He thought about the last ten years or so and the moment he found out his wife and father in law were funding piracy. How he checked their bank accounts and found millions of pounds in other accounts. How he had been told, by an informed source, they were going to kill him while he was racing in the Americas cup. How the "Bettesworth Switch" was set up by his source and after his attack he was to dive under the hull and make for the sealed pod with its own air supply.

How it all went to plan until Whitcombe found his hiding place. They knew that someone else knew of their plan as the Bettesworth switch had been set up. This convinced them to keep him alive in case they needed a hostage. He then spent the next ten years being held in captivity by his wife and his father in law. He knew one day the source would spring him, and when it happened on the island of Socotra, had no remorse for the demise of his mentally unstable wife and her totally doting father.

He thought about the time he had missed from his family their three children together.

Andrew, now thirty years old, was an upper class snob, who took a first at Cambridge in Law and now, had his own, law firm. He was the most objectionable person and did not have a kind word for anyone. Needless to say father and son did not get on.

His middle son Mark now twenty seven years old, had attended University obtained a degree in Physics and then enlisted with the Royal Marines. He was now a Captain and had been the apple of his father's eye.

Their only daughter Elizabeth was twenty four years old and again had obtained a degree at Cambridge in History and worked at the Victoria and Albert Museum as a trainee curator. She had been fourteen years old when Anderson was kidnapped and she had missed her father dreadfully.

Anderson would never forgive his wife for what she did in making him miss watching them grow.

Felix was back in Lymington in March 2010 with Belle and they were enjoying their time together, relaxing they even managed some spring sailing and slowly the whole thing seemed to have been just a dream. They were sent a thank you and a congratulatory letters from both Sir Henry and The Prime Minister. Felix received a promotion and was put forward for a decoration in the New Year's Honour's list. Belle was given a Senior Post in the Geology unit of the Department of The Environment. She also told Felix he was to become a father for the first time. They were both over the moon. They had grown as people over the last year or so and this was another new challenge they relished. Felix sat with Belle on the harbour wall watching the Isle of Wight car ferry warily make its way towards the harbour mouth.

"I love this harbour" said Felix. "But I love you even more Mrs Barnard" he said as he put his arms around her "And my place will always be with you."

"Life is going to be incredibly dull from now on." she sighed.

"Well it may not be as dull as you think my darling." said Felix smiling.

"What do you mean by that?" She replied.

"Felix took a letter from his pocket and opened it up" It appears my darling we are now one point two million pounds better off so the world is our lobster." He laughed.

"You mean oyster." she giggled.

"Well some crustaceans anyhow." he roared

"You shellfish prawn." she shrieked her eyes watering with laughter.

"Who is this windfall from?" asked Belle.

"Call it a finder's fee" said Felix.

"I always fancied a home on a deserted sandy beach." she said.

"Name the place and its yours my lovely."

They both looked at each other.

"As long as we have each other we could live anywhere." Felix sighed.

"We could my darling but our child will need a home." she said with mock seriousness.

"Anabella Barnard you are absolutely gorgeous." he bowed.

"By the way we have been offered a cottage free of charge on the Rowlands Castle Estate whenever we want it." Belle said out of the blue.

"And what's the catch?" said Felix suspiciously.

"Apparently we have friends in high places." laughed Belle.

"Things are looking up." agreed Felix.

Sir Henry met with the Prime Minister in his Downing Street office.

"All's well that ends well Henry." said the PM smiling.

"Yes Richard." agreed Henry.

"Did we manage to trace the millions they made?" Asked the PM.

"Only a small amount Sir, it seems it came in and went straight out again." replied Henry.

"Apart from Wincanton and his daughter, can we recoup that?"

"Yes Sir." replied Henry.

"How much?" Asked the PM.

"About five million pounds." said Henry.

"What shall we do with it?" Asked the PM.

"I thought we should donate it to *Homes for our Heroes.*"

"Brilliant Idea Henry" smiled the PM.

Danielle Chambers was chairing the meeting of the Patrons of the charity

"I have some really good news." she said. "We have received an anonymous donation of five million pounds."

There was spontaneous applause from all of the members of the board.

"This is brilliant news." said Brigadier Handley "Although you say its anonymous can we be certain it comes from a reliable source?"

"I can assure you Brigadier, it has come from the most reliable and trustworthy source" Danielle replied.

After the meeting she went through the Charities accounts with the Auditors and the total fund after expenses had been deducted exceeded eight million pounds. The auditor smiled at Danielle.

"Your charity is by far the most popular for public support I have ever known."

"It's because it's for our brave boys and girls." she smiled at the auditor.

He shook her hand and said "Your books all balance. I congratulate you and your team."

Sir Henry sat in his study running things over in his mind. How much money had been made: according to his analysts fifty million and they had recovered only five million. Someone has made a fortune he mused but how would they be able to cover up such a huge amount of money?

"By putting it where there were already large sums of money" he said out loud.

He picked up his phone and said "Andrew I want you to do me a favour."

After he explained what he wanted the voice at the other end of the phone said "Leave it with me Henry."

Sir Henry put the phone down and smiled. If ever there was a solicitor who was honest Henry had not met him yet.

The voice was smiling smugly, things could not have gone better the idiots used to set up the initial contacts in the business world and the military world were all dead. It appeared that all parties were happy with apparent outcome.

The piracy from Devils Cove had now stopped and four hostages and many sailing vessels had been returned to their rightful owners.

A military charity had benefitted to the tune of five million.

Tony had been released and was free to live his life as he pleased.

And lastly, but certainly not least, the voice was forty five million better off.

A sum of three million had been made available to Tony to facilitate his new life. Felix Barnard had actually been a fortunate intervention as it turned out; in another two years it would be the life of dreams, long since planned away, from this cold, damp country full of self-righteous hypocrites.

Danielle Chambers added a new numbered account to the five hundred she already had in Swiss, Oman, Quatar and Cuban accounts. She also had special accounts with Libyan Banks and had a large diamond collection in Amsterdam. She had purchased large quantities of gold via intermediaries and had this in various deposit boxes in banks around the world. All these accounts were registered as off shore companies.

Give it a couple of years and she would be off.

"Leave this idiot of a husband, politicians are all the same" she thought. "Except Tony. He was gorgeous, but even he had this thing about saving the country. When he told her what his wife and Wincanton where up to she suddenly saw a chance to make money.

She used Tony's contacts to muscle in on the whole operation. They thought they were working for their hero. Eventually she took over the running of all aspects of business without them knowing who she was. It was all so easy.

As a bonus it meant having the woman who had been shagging her husband for the last ten years killed in the process. Not that she cared she had got over that years ago but it was just icing on the cake.

Tony was reading the Times when he read about the mystery donation to the *"Homes for the Heroes"* charity. He smiled to himself "Well done Danni as good as your word. It has all been worthwhile if all the ill-gotten gains have made their way into a charity set up to support service personnel" he said. aloud. He then read on and read the account of the Auditors report regarding the assets of the charity at just over eight million pounds.

"That can't be right" he said he read the article again and slowly it started to sink in.

"So you played me like a sap" he said fuming.

Anderson picked up the phone and when it was answered said" We need to meet urgently" he listened to the reply and said "I will be there."

He then made another three calls one for justice one for love and the third for money.

Danielle met Anderson at the delightful village of Old Bosham just east of Chichester Sussex. They walked along the tidal road at the water's edge.

"What can I do for you Tony?" smiled Danielle.

"You lied to me Danni." he said quietly.

"You said all this was about stopping their illegal activities" he went on" and any monies they made were to be given to service charities." he looked straight at her "Isn't that what we agreed?"

"Oh Tony Tony." she sighed "That is exactly what I have done." she said.

"What about the other thirty million?" he asked.

"Call it my handling charge darling." she smiled again.

"I have put three million in a numbered account for you. Call it out of pocket expenses."

"The money has driven you mad Danni. Just as it did to Vicky."

"Don't you dare compare me with that sad excuse for a woman." she flared. "I was the one who saw the possibilities of this opportunity. They had not seen the possibilities of the insurance and shipping businesses. It doubled the profit margins."

She stopped suddenly sensing she was losing her self-control.

"Anyway you have got exactly what you wanted." she carried on now back in control. "Firstly you got rid of that horrendous wife and her cranky father. Then you have got five million for the charity closest to your heart." she sighed "And finally you get three million to do what you like from now on." she stopped and then added "Can't be bad can it?"

Tony could not help himself from smiling.

"What are you going to do with thirty million Danni?"

"Spend it." she said turning her back on him.

"Give it back Danni by all means keep five million but give the rest back."

She turned to face him "Sorry Tony I can't do that" she was holding a Smith and Wesson pistol in her hand.

"I actually think I loved you Tony I thought you were different, but you are all the same underneath you have no vision."

Tony never moved he looked straight at her "You will have to kill me Danni."

She glanced up and down the deserted tidal road.

"I am afraid you are right" she pulled the trigger and shot him straight through the heart and he fell to the floor.

"Put the gun down Danni" said a voice she knew well.

"I have three snipers sights trained on you as we speak" said her husband the countries Prime Minister from his position in a garden overlooking the road.

"It's all over" he said

"Fuck you!" she said but before she could fire the snipers took her out.

The Prime Minister and Sir Henry stepped down onto the road and looked down at the two bodies; the prime minister's wife and an ex-prime minister both dead.

The PM turned to the SAS Officer "Clear these up Captain."

"Yes sir." he replied.

The PM walked off with Sir Henry.

He turned to Henry and said

"Well at least there are no loose ends"

Henry said quietly. "Sorry about Danni."

The PM looked back as he was about to get into his waiting car shrugged his shoulders and said "Collateral damage Henry." and then he closed the door and his car drove off.

Sir Henry walked back to his chauffer driven Jaguar and climbed in.

"Take me home George" he sighed.

He picked up his scrambled car phone.

"Hello Andrew did you manage to trace those accounts?" he asked.

"Yes Henry most of them anyway." he replied.

"Excellent work, have the transfers been completed?" He asked.

"All completed today to the accounts specified Henry." he replied.

"You are going to be a very rich man Andrew Anderson" said Henry.

"I am looking forward to it." he said.

"I will be in touch." said Henry.

After he put the phone down he was thinking of the money that the refurbishment of his country home cost him, but it was all worth it.

Once he heard of the missing millions he used Anderson's eldest son to use his family connections to trace the missing accounts. He had obviously been involved in at least some of the transactions to invest his mothers and grandfathers ill-gotten gains so Henry felt no guilt in tidying up. He picked up the phone again "Hello Perseus I have a little job for you." he said. He put the phone down looked out the window and to no one in particular he said "All tied up now."

Meanwhile back at the now partly flooded road at Bosham a Royal Marines Captain on attachment to the SAS picked the body of Anthony Anderson up and looked him in the eye and said.

"Welcome home dad." and the two hugged unashamedly.

Anderson looked admiringly at his son.

"Great to see you Mark." He put his arm round his dad's shoulders and smiled.

"Liz is in the car dad it's time to be a family again."

Anthony Anderson smiled the nightmare was over.

"Thank god Danni was a good shot this bulletproof vest would have been useless if she had aimed at my head." His son smiled.

"You always liked to gamble Dad."

They were joined by his daughter Liz who hugged him and said.

"Welcome home dad I have prayed for this day for years."

"So have I my darling." And they all walked off arm in arm.

The SAS attachment had been promised free booze by Mark and Anderson and they now had to keep to their word.

"By the way dad, Andrew traced a lot of the money for Sir Henry as you suspected." said Mark

"But not all of it." said Anderson smiling broadly.

EPILOGUE

Felix and Belle bought a four bedroom detached cottage at Dell Quay on the edge of Chichester Harbour. It was about five minutes' walk to the to the quay itself and nestling next to the quay was the Crown and Anchor a family pub with a large garden area looking out to sea. As it was very tidal *Vida Nova* was moored at the nearby Old Bosham harbour. Their first child Martin was quickly followed by another Carly and they had an idyllic lifestyle.

About two years after they moved in Felix was asked to visit Whitehall to look as some design work on a modern hoist. When he arrived he was met by two familiar faces. One was the newly promoted Colonel David Fuller and the other was the also newly promoted Colonel Michael Mathews.

"How are the injuries?" Felix asked Michael.

"Last time I saw you, you were in a hospital bed." He added.

He put out his hand and shook Felix's warmly.

"If it hadn't been for that intuition of yours we would all have been dead." he said smiling broadly.

David Fuller also shook his hand warmly.

"I know what you mean Michael. I have seen this guy in action, it's amazing what six weeks at Hereford can do."

Felix was so pleased to see these two guys who had put their life on the line to save Belle and he felt he owed them.

"Alright" he said. "You haven't dragged me down here to reminisce have you?" He said smiling.

"I am shocked." said David looking at Michael.

"As if we had an ulterior motive." said Michael sounding hurt.

"Come on guys what's the score?"

They both laughed out loud "Alright it's a fair cop" said David raising his hands.

"We want you to work for us in Military Intelligence." Before Felix could say a word he continued.

"You would attend Dartmouth Officer Training College for twelve weeks, but the training would be carried out by a team of specialists."

Felix was still too shocked to say a word so Michael chipped in.

"Once you have successfully completed your training you will pass out as a Lieutenant in Her Majesties Royal Navy."

"And then" said David smugly "You will join us in defence of your country."

"I need time to think this over I don't know if I could do it." Felix whimpered.

"We know you have already have done it and you did it bloody well too." David smiled.

"If we didn't think you could handle it, you would not be here Felix." added Michael.

Felix left their office and headed home not sure how he was going to tell Belle what they had offered him. He plumped for the head on approach.

"Darling I have been offered a commission in the Royal Navy but I will be working for Military Intelligence."

She smiled at him and took his hands.

"I had never ever seen you as alive as you were during our adventure. It came so naturally to you and you were very good at it too. I am alive because of you." She said proudly.

She put her arms around him and added "I have always had a thing for a man in a uniform."

"That's agreed then." Felix said.

"Now where has that Scuba diving suit gone?" he laughed.

Anthony Anderson returned to his Rowlands Castle home and used his influence to arrange a new identity, such as passport, a new NI Number and within six months he was even asked to stand for the County Council Elections. An offer he declined, once bitten twice shy.

Through his contacts in the Far East had traced a lot of gold bullion and a serious amount of diamonds from his colleagues in Brussels and Amsterdam. He estimated that he had recovered around twelve million pounds sterling allowing for the loss in handling and for ensuring they were not traceable.

He slowly fed the money into charities and organisations that he felt supported the British way of life. His father had died of Cancer and therefore the local cancer charities and the Rowans Hospice, where his father had passed away, was continually receiving anonymous donations. Although he had been a man with the world at his feet and who had been completely at ease in the public eye. His ten year forced imprisonment had changed his outlook on life. He was happy to spend time with his children and do the normal things that families do.

He did spend some money on himself. He bought a wooden hulled thirty foot motor sailing yacht that was in need of repair. He paid £5,000 cash for it from a local yacht builder in Lymington. He spent nearly a year and another £10,000 rebuilding it until it was totally restored. He sailed it around the Isle of Wight and along the coast to Cornwall. But once it was completed he seemed to lose interest so he gave it to Mark as he was now a keen sailor. He then went back to the same Lymington boatyard and the owner offered him a job restoring the traditional yachts that need a craftsman's hands to repair.

He met the owners daughter one day and they had a long discussion regarding sailing craft and racing around these shores. She was so impressed with his knowledge, she asked if he would like to come to dinner one evening and meet her husband. So Felix and Belle had dinner with Anthony Christian, and they soon became firm friends. He had picked his new surname, Christian, after the fairy story author Hans Christian Anderson.

He did not attend the funeral of his eldest son Andrew who was tragically killed in a road accident on the edges of Epping Forest.

Sir Henry Waddington Walker managed to trace over ten million pounds, or at least Andrew Anderson did, and this was to be invested in Finchdean Hall his family's home since the early eighteenth century. There was still dry rot in several bedrooms and the floor of the library needed a complete replacement. He would now be able to replace the whole floor with well-seasoned oak.

He had arranged for Andrew to have a road accident as he was up to his neck in his mother's business.

He was not surprised that the PM wanted Victoria disposed of as he was aware of their clandestine affair. This may come in handy for later he thought.

His next big task was to ensure he was elected PM. To this end all the information he had collated on his top cabinet colleagues would ensure this became a reality.

His home and his personal advancement had both been winners in this unfortunate incident.

His manservant Williams knocked and then entered his study. "Sorry to interrupt you sir, this came in by the post for you."

A box carrying the logo of a furniture restorer was placed before him. "You did tell me not to put any of these items through the security screening."

"That's fine Williams this will be another restored item for the library." He opened the heavy duty wax covering and took out a hand carved jade dagger. "This is absolutely beautiful" he said staring at the totally restored item.

"That will be all Williams" he said. Williams closed the door quietly. He was looking at the dagger when a piece of paper caught his eye in the box.

He opened the folded note. "Hope you enjoy your trophy you traitor." It was signed Vicky.

Sir Henry suddenly panicked and made to run for the door but the explosive in the base of the package ruined both his restoration and his life.

Richard Chambers was happy with his life; he had survived what could have been a difficult time for him personally and politically.

Vicky and her father were both dead so he had no more obligations to the family. Anderson was also dead, not that he had any idea he had been shagging his wife for years, or of his involvement with the insider trading he arranged for the Wincanton family.

He did not miss his wife Danni in the least, their marriage had been a sham for the last ten years. She was the perfect host for social functions and came from the right background to further his career.

He did miss the special sex games with Vicky at the stable block at Chertsey so he was pleasantly surprised when the stables owner enquired whether he would like to train a new filly, obviously under the same strict confidential terms. This was the proverbial icing on the cake so he agreed to start the training that Friday evening.

Everything was exactly as before except the new filly, a twenty four year old blonde with large breasts had replaced Vicky. She was wearing the same halter and the same harness, with a rubber bit in her mouth and leather straps between her breasts. The final piece was a leather strap around her waist to which a horse's tail was attached. Apart from these items she was naked. Richard started by using the lunge rein, a long rein and she had to walk, trot and canter on command. If she made a mistake she had to be punished using a rubber whip. When the training was over she was led to the end stable where she was shagged continually over each stable door.

Life can't get any better he thought as his driver drove him home.

The full spread photos made the Sunday press and the whole episode was filmed and released on U Tube the same day.

Richard Chambers stepped down as Prime Minister the following Tuesday and was not reselected by his constituency party at the next election.

He received a letter some weeks later from Vicky, dated six months previous.

Which said "You may have fucked me for years but now I've fucked you for good!"

Printed and bound by CPI Group (UK) Ltd, Croydon, CR0 4YY